Lottie Loser

A Contemporary Romance Novel

Dana L. Brown

Lottie Loser

A Contemporary Romance Novel

Dana L. Brown

AMI Series Book 1

Published by:
Southern Yellow Pine (SYP) Publishing
4351 Natural Bridge Rd.
Tallahassee, FL 32305

www.syppublishing.com

This is a work of fiction. Names, characters, places, and events that occur either are the products of the author's imagination or are used fictitiously. Any resemblance to actual persons, places, or events is purely coincidental.

The contents and opinions expressed in this book do not necessarily reflect the views and opinions of Southern Yellow Pine Publishing, nor does the mention of brands or trade names constitute endorsement.

ISBN-13: 978-1-59616-048-4
ISBN-13: ePub 978-1-59616-049-1
ISBN-13: Adobe PDF eBook 978-1-59616-060-6
Library of Congress Control Number: 2018931420

Printed in the United States of America
First SYP Publishing Edition
January 2018

This book is dedicated to my happily ever after, my husband Bob and our three amazing daughters, Jenifer, Torey, and Alison. Your love and support have made my fairytale come true.

Praise for the Author

A true page turner!!! From the first page the reader is transported into the mind of Charlotte, a fascinating and totally relatable character. Through emotionally charged details, Charlotte, a strong and independent woman, allows you a peak into her well-hidden vulnerabilities.

I have special praise for the author's ability to weave the past and present in such a way that it keeps you wanting more. In this national award-winning contemporary romance, you will be hooked on Lottie. Can't wait for the second book in this captivating series!

K. I. Knight, Author of the national award-winning series *"Fate & Freedom"*

Lottie Loser is a feel-good contemporary romance. With relatable characters, an enjoyable plot, and gentle humor, Lottie Loser is a page-turning read.

Melanie Thurlow, Author of *Rose by Another Name, The Blythe Series*

A thoroughly engaging romance where the characters jump off the pages and capture your heart. Read Dana L. Brown!"

Colleen Connally, Amazon Best Selling Author; *Secret Lives Series, Boston's Crimes of Passion Series, The Three Realms Series*

Lottie Loser is a fresh, compelling story about second chances, rekindled love, and finding yourself. The characters were relatable- in fact, I think women everywhere will relate to Lottie in some way. I already can't wait to read it again!

April Hughes, The *Vagaries of Us* blog.

LOTTIE LOSER is a gripping love story of a young woman's struggle to overcome the past and build a new life for herself on a beautiful tropical island off the coast of Florida. What she doesn't expect is for the past to catch up with her, and things sizzle and pop to the last riveting page!

David C. Edmonds, multiple award-winning author of *Lily of Peru and The Girl in the Glyphs*

Chapter 1

Now

Charcoal pencil skirt, white Prada blouse, black Manolo heels—the outfit that always made her confidence as solid as her title. But today neither the designer clothes nor the name she read every morning on her office door was helping.

"I'm Charlotte Luce," she reminded herself, "first female market president of Olde Florida Bank and the youngest in the bank's one hundred years' history, and I can do this." *Right,* she thought with a sigh. *I can tell the best man I've ever known, the closest thing to a father figure I had growing up, that the bank will be foreclosing on his property in ninety days if his payments aren't brought up to date.*

She plastered on her best smile and gave herself one last look in the mirror. Before stepping out the door, she fastened her silver locket around her neck and wished once more that she could talk to her gran. Gran had always known when Charlotte needed her and had always known just what to say, which was why she had given Charlotte the locket for her college graduation. The inscription "Whither thou goest, I will go," taken from the book of Ruth, was Gran's way of telling Charlotte she would always be with her. Charlotte put the locket on the last thing every morning and always lifted up a prayer to the grandmother she had adored.

"Thank you for always believing in me, Gran," she whispered, "and give me the strength I need to make it through this day." With that she grabbed her suit jacket and headed out the door.

Charlotte swirled the cold coffee in her cup and looked at the clock again. A normal Monday morning would go by in a rush of e-mails, customer calls, and paperwork, but today the clock was taunting her and drawing out her agony.

One of the strawberry-blonde curls that she had so professionally secured on top of her head was trying to break free. Just as she was about to pin it back in place, her phone rang. Between her nerves and the loud buzz of the phone, Charlotte jumped and pulled the errant curl even farther out of place. "Yes?" Charlotte said into the phone, knowing what her assistant, Carol, was going to say but acting as nonchalant as possible.

"Mr. Nicholas Greyson to see you," Carol said very formally, and Charlotte sighed again. She pushed the curl back in place and was just about to stand when Carol opened the door and ushered the client inside. With one more silent prayer of courage to Gran, Charlotte stood up, and holy crap, there he stood.

Not Nicholas Greyson her customer, whose marina was in financial trouble and about to be foreclosed on, not the Nicholas Greyson who had been there for her every time her mother had not, but Nicholas Greyson Jr., the boy whom she had fallen in love with when she was nine and who had broken her heart when she was seventeen. And there he was standing in her office, all six feet five inches of molten masculinity, and for a moment the world stood still.

It had been twelve years since the last time they had seen each other, the night their friendship had come crashing down, and it was taking everything she had to stay focused. To say he looked incredible was an understatement. With his navy sports coat and perfectly cut trousers that hugged his muscular thighs, rich brown hair that Charlotte used to tell him reminded her of the good chocolate Gran always had at Christmastime, and eyes the color of the deep blue ocean, Nick was hot. Scorching hot. She closed her eyes just for a second to come up with the right opening, but Nick spoke first.

2

"Hello, Lottie," he said softly. "You look—"

"Thinner, yes, I hear that a lot," Charlotte retorted a little sharper than she intended, "and it's Charlotte now. Lottie's been gone a long time."

She took a breath and smiled, but she could see the hurt in his eyes. The expression on his face never changed, but even after all these years, Charlotte could see the way his blue eyes darkened, and for Nick that always meant he was hurt but not about to show it. That little bit of knowledge was enough to throw her off guard, and she wasn't prepared for Nick's next comment.

"Well," he said with a sly smirk on his face, "I was going to say all grown-up, but whatever. You look good, um, Charlotte."

Charlotte felt her ears get red and then decided to take control of the situation. "I don't believe you're a current customer of Olde Florida's, Nick, so if you're here to open an account, I'll take you back to Carol, and she'll be happy to help you."

Open an account? Couldn't I have come up with something better than that? Charlotte silently berated herself. For the past twelve years she had thought so many times about what she would say to Nick if she ever saw him again, and asking if he wanted to open an account was the best she could do?

Nick moved toward her desk and sat down in a chair across from it. "I have a ten a.m. appointment with you, Lott—I mean Charlotte. If you'll look at your calendar, I'm sure you'll see it there. Go ahead; I have the time."

Why, the arrogant jerk! she thought. *This is my office, and I'm the president. Who does he think he is?* But of course Olde Florida lived by the motto of Customers First, so she swallowed and as gracefully as possible asked, "What can I do for you, Nick?"

"I'm here to help my dad." Five short words, but what an impact they had.

Charlotte sat down. She knew Nick wasn't going to like what she told him next, so she was trying to make the playing field equal. "I can't discuss your dad's business with you, Nick, unless he's here to approve it. Privacy laws just don't allow it. I'm sure you can appreciate that?"

3

There, that was how a market president behaved. The ball was back in her court. For about two seconds.

Nick opened his jacket, and there it was, the proof behind the stories Charlotte had heard. A gun was holstered close to his waist, and she would have pushed her security button except for the gold shield beside the gun, letting her know that the man in front of her, her childhood friend Nick, the boy she had loved and ultimately hated, was now Special Agent Nicholas Greyson, Federal Bureau of Investigation.

Chapter 2

Then

Today was math, and Lottie couldn't wait! She loved numbers and knew she was the best math student in the class. Gran told her that she needed to be humble with her God-given abilities, but Lottie had skipped the fourth grade because she was such a strong student, and she had heard the principal, Mr. Royston, tell her mom that she could truthfully move up to the sixth grade, even though he didn't recommend it. For once Mom had listened to someone in authority, so Lottie at age nine was in the fifth grade with the ten- and eleven-year-olds.

She was just putting away her English book when there was a knock on the classroom door. Mrs. Walsh went out into the hall and returned a few minutes later with a boy, and just as Lottie looked up, he smiled at her.

"Class." Mrs. Walsh softly clapped her hands to get their attention. "We have a new student to welcome to Island View, Nick Greyson, who moved all the way here from New York City. I know you will all make him feel at home, right? Now let's see; we need to get you a desk buddy."

At Island View, desks were designed for two students, and at the beginning of the year, Mrs. Walsh had allowed everyone to choose his or her desk buddy. As long as there wasn't horseplay or too much talking, she didn't make changes to the seating assignment. Because

Lottie was at least a year younger than the rest of the students, she didn't have any real friends in the class, which had left half of her desk empty.

"I'd be more than happy to be Nicky's desk buddy," purred perfect little Ashley Marshall. With her silky, blonde curls and fancy outfits from *Justice*, Ashley was the most popular girl in the fifth grade, but she had never given Lottie the time of day.

"That's very generous of you, Ashley," replied Mrs. Walsh, "but Lea is just out sick today, so she'll be needing her seat tomorrow when she comes back. Nick, let's put you back here with Lottie."

Mrs. Walsh walked the newcomer past Ashley to the last row and showed him where to sit. He gave Lottie another crooked smile and announced boldly to the class, "My name's Nick, not Nicky."

Lottie looked over and saw the red creeping up Ashley's neck.

Years later, way after "the incident" with Nick, she realized it was at that moment in fifth grade that Ashley Marshall had made Lottie public enemy number one.

Chapter 3

Now

For a couple of seconds, though it seemed more like hours, the office was silent, and then Nick handed her a document. She looked it over carefully before speaking.

"Power of attorney papers, Nick?" she questioned. "Is your dad okay?" The thought that Mr. Greyson might be sick or suffering from some kind of memory ailment broke her heart, but it also might help to make sense of what had happened with his finances.

"Dad's fine, at least physically," Nick replied. "Emotionally he's as confused as the rest of us as to what's going on at the marina, which is why I've come home to help. Now, as you can see, everything has been notarized and is legal, so can we cut to the chase and talk about what's going on?"

Charlotte could see the frustration in his face, and for a minute her heart softened. *How like Nick to come back when his dad needs him,* she thought. *He's a good man.* But then quickly her mind shot back to the August after their senior year, and all her good feelings flew out the window.

Carefully choosing her words, Charlotte said, "Your dad's in financial trouble, Nick, but obviously you know that. I was going to tell him today at what I thought was our appointment that the bank can't give him any more time and that foreclosure proceedings will start if he can't catch up his payments."

Charlotte looked at Nick, expecting him to argue or yell. What she didn't expect was for him to pull a cashier's check for $150,000 out of his pocket and lay it on her desk. "Will this be enough to satisfy you, Charlotte?" he asked, giving her that same crooked smile he always gave when he knew he had the upper hand.

"Where did this come from, Nick?" she asked, genuinely surprised. "This is over half of your dad's debt."

"Does it matter where it came from as long as it's good? But since you asked so nicely, and I know how much you care about my dad, I borrowed from my 401(k). Satisfied? Now, will you please call off your henchmen?"

This was not the confrontation she wanted with Nick, and she was genuinely thrilled for his dad. Instead of replying, she buzzed Carol and asked her to step into the office. As soon as the door opened, Nick stood, and Carol's southern belle kicked in.

"Why, what a gentleman you are, Mr. Greyson," she fawned, "but then I believe you're Noah Greyson's brother, and he's a gentleman too. We went out a couple of times this past year. Maybe he mentioned me?"

"Ah, Carol," Charlotte cut in, "I need for you to get this POA paper scanned into our system and prepare new signature cards today that are titled the same way. That's all, thanks."

Knowing she was being dismissed, Carol gave Nick her brightest smile and left the room.

"If you and your dad want to stop by later today and sign the paperwork," Charlotte said, standing up, "you'll have access to all of your dad's financial records. I really do hope you get to the bottom of this, Nick. Your dad is one of my favorite people in the world."

Apparently, that was the opening he was looking for, as he said, "Then why don't you bring the paperwork to the marina this afternoon? You can see him, and we can sign the new cards. I know he'd love to see you." Nick looked up at her, and Charlotte felt a pang in her heart. She wanted to see Mr. Greyson, and she missed going to the marina, but she had never wanted the problem with Nick to come up, so she had just stayed away. She saw Mr. Greyson in the bank and around town, of course, but it had been twelve years since she had stepped foot in the place that had once been her second home.

"I'm really busy today, Nick," she tried to explain. "I have Rotary at noon and a client appointment in Sarasota at three, so…"

"Perfect, stop by after Sarasota. Pop's frying grouper and making peach ice cream!" She was all ready to say no when Nick threw in the sinker. "It would mean the world to him," he said softly, and she knew she was had.

"All right, I'll stop by after my appointment in Sarasota, but I don't want dinner, and I don't eat peach ice cream anymore. You can both sign the paperwork, and I'll save you a trip back to town."

A genuine smile came across Nick's face, and as he turned to leave, he winked. "See you later, Lottie, and thanks!"

"It's Charlotte," she called after him and then sat down in her chair and put her head in her hands. "What kind of deal with the devil did I just make?"

Chapter 4

Then

The rest of the afternoon was devoted to math, but Lottie couldn't begin to concentrate. She had a desk buddy, and a new boy at that! When Mrs. Walsh called on her for an answer, something that Lottie knew as well as her own name, she was tongue-tied, and the rest of the class laughed. Everyone except Nick—not Nicky, but Nick. He gave her the same smile that he had when he'd first seen her, and for some reason the laughing didn't hurt so much. She wanted to smile back, but just looking at him made her blush, and she knew with her red hair and pale skin, a blush was more like a sunburn than just pink cheeks.

Finally, it was time for recess, and Lottie couldn't wait to find her friend Becca, who was in the fourth grade, to tell her all about Nick! Just as she was getting up from her seat, Nick asked her, "So what do you do during recess around here?" A simple question, but again Lottie was tongue-tied.

"Well," she stammered, "you can play kickball or shoot hoops or just hang out, I guess."

"What do you do?" Nick responded.

"I play kickball," Lottie said, "but with the fourth-grade class. Most of the fifth-grade boys play HORSE, and I'm sure they'd let you join in."

"Maybe tomorrow, but today I want to play kickball. Lead the way!"

Lottie had never felt so special or on display in her life! Everyone seemed to be looking at her, but she wasn't sure it was in a good way.

Ashley walked by with her group of stuck-up fifth-grade girls and linked her arm through Nick's. "Nick," she said sweetly, "why don't you come over here and let little Lottie play with her little friends. I'd love to hear all about New York City and why you moved to Anna Maria."

Lottie started to walk away, but she heard Nick's response to Ashley. "New York's just another place to live," he told her. "I'm here because this is where my dad is, and kickball with Lottie's friends sounds like fun to me." And with that he turned back to Lottie, and this time when he smiled at her, she didn't blush.

Chapter 5

Now

The Rotary meeting was long, and the drive to Sarasota was slow, so by the time Charlotte was headed to the marina, she was tired, hot, and scared shitless! "How did I end up in this position?" she asked herself for the tenth time. She did not want to go to the marina, the happiest place of her childhood, and relive the old memories that she had worked so hard to suppress, but most of all, she did not want to see Nick!

Twelve years had gone by since their high school graduation, but Charlotte could still feel the hurt and humiliation of that August night as if it were yesterday. She had worked so hard, in college and in her job, to reinvent herself from that five-foot-ten-inch, chubby girl with frizzy, red hair and big boobs to the trim, stylish, five-foot-ten-inch woman with wavy hair who knew how to dress for her curvy figure. Seeing Nick today brought all the memories and all the old insecurities tumbling back. He had been her best friend and her first love, but it had been secret love that only Becca had known about. Somehow, though, those last few weeks before the incident, Charlotte had felt things change between her and Nick, and unfortunately, she had let wishful thinking get in the way of logic. Nick had become one of the most popular guys in school, an all-state swimmer with the broad shoulders and strong thighs of an athlete and the face of an Abercrombie model, so why would she have ever thought he would think of her as more than a friend? But she had let her heart lead her, and it had led right into a heartbreak that "all the kings' horses and all the kings' men," couldn't put back together again. So just like Humpty Dumpty she was broken, at least on the inside, and she still didn't know how to move on.

She pulled into the marina parking lot and automatically reached for her locket. "Oh, Gran," she whispered, "I need your help. I honestly don't think I can do this." At just that moment Charlotte heard her name called, and her face lit up with a huge smile. She opened the car door and took off running without even bothering to shut it.

"Noah," she squealed, "is it really you?"

Noah lifted her off the ground and twirled her in his strong arms.

"I didn't know you were going to be here," she laughed. "When did you get back?"

Noah's response was to give her a big kiss, and the two of them held on to each other, hugging and laughing like kids.

As Charlotte turned back to close her car door, the loud sound of a throat being cleared grabbed her attention, and she glanced up to see Nick leaning against the door to the house, his arms crossed over his chest and a less-than-happy expression on his face. But Charlotte didn't care, and Noah was obviously not fazed, because he ruffled her hair and kissed the top of her head.

"Oh, Lottie," Noah said with a smile, "it's so good to see you."

Charlotte and Noah walked arm in arm right past Nick as he was trying to tell his brother, "It's Charlotte," but neither paid any attention to him, which seemed to just downright piss him off.

But it was when Charlotte came face-to-face with their dad, in the kitchen she had always loved, that a feeling of peace came over her. She walked right into his arms.

"Welcome back, Lottie," he said as he hugged the young woman whom he loved like a daughter. "This old place just hasn't been the same without you."

Charlotte looked at the three men standing before her and couldn't believe how good they all looked nor how much she had missed them. Noah was almost as tall as Nick, but his hair was longer and bleached blond by his days on a fishing boat. His brown eyes, his legacy from

13

his mother, still twinkled with mischief, and she was pretty certain his earlier display of affection had been meant to rankle his big brother. Noah and Lottie were the same age and had always been good friends, but friendship was all it had ever been. Nick's dad was in his mid-fifties, and not quite as tall as his sons, but to her he was every bit as handsome. He and Nick had the same blue eyes, but his dark hair was peppered with white now. Charlotte was so lost in thought that she almost missed Nick's question.

"I need a clarification, please," he stated angrily. "I have to call you Charlotte, but to these two you answer to Lottie?"

Charlotte felt bad for about two seconds and then replied with a smirk, "What can I say, Nick? I love these guys." She gave him the biggest smile she could muster and thought, *Way to go, girl! Coming here may not have been a mistake after all.*

Chapter 6

Then

By the end of the day Lottie had met Nick's brother, Noah, who was in the fourth grade with her friend Becca, and the four of them were headed to the marina that Nick and Noah's dad owned. Anna Maria was small and safe enough that the girls usually walked home from school and stopped for ice cream at Two Scoops, so Becca knew her mom wouldn't worry. Lottie knew her mom wouldn't care.

"Wow!" exclaimed Becca. "I've lived here my whole life, and I never knew the marina was anything besides a place to store boats! I can't believe you not only live here but have a store and a snack bar right at your fingertips!"

The boys just shrugged their shoulders. "We just got here last week," Noah replied. "This is all we know."

About that time a man who looked like a grown-up version of Nick came into the store. "Well, hello there," he said with a smile, "I'm Nicholas Greyson, the father of these two rogues, but most people call me Pop. Would you lovely ladies care for a soda or a glass of freshly squeezed lemonade?"

Lottie was in awe. She had grown up without a father, and here was one not only home after school but also offering them drinks? Becca had a dad—Lottie had even met him—but he was usually working or coaching Becca's brother in some sport, not spending time with them, so all this attention caused Lottie to do what she did best: blush. If he noticed, Mr. Greyson didn't say anything. He simply moved behind the snack bar to get the drinks.

From that day forward, after-school visits to the marina became a ritual, and Lottie found out what it meant to have an adult, other than Gran, in her life whom she could trust and feel safe with.

Chapter 7

Now

After Noah caught Charlotte up about his adventures captaining his commercial fishing boat, Mr. Greyson suggested a swim before dinner. "Oh no," Charlotte replied, shaking her head, "I'm not staying to eat, Mr. Greyson, and of course I didn't bring a bathing suit."

"Not staying to eat?" Mr. Greyson put his hand over his heart like he was wounded. "I'm fixing grilled grouper and peach ice cream, all of your favorites. And don't you think it's time you called me Pop again? Mr. Greyson is your customer; Pop is your friend."

Charlotte blushed, of course, but didn't have the heart to tell him that she didn't eat fried food or ice cream anymore, because more than anything she wanted Pop back in her life. "Okay, I'll stay."

Noah chimed in, "I know that Maya left some suits here. I'll get you one of hers, and we can have a swim before dinner just like the old days!"

Charlotte groaned. Maya was the guy's older and much smaller sister, probably a perfect size 6. Even with Charlotte's weight loss, her chest was nowhere near a size 6, but how did she tell that to three men? "Uh, really, I'll just sit here and talk with you, Pop," she said, hoping her use of his nickname would get her off the hook, but no!

"Nonsense, Lottie," he laughed. "You get out there and have some fun, and that's an order!"

Charlotte looked up to see a gleam in Nick's eyes. He'd stayed pretty quiet while she'd talked with his brother and dad, but he of all people knew her discomfort with her body image, and now he was going to get some revenge for being ignored. "Come on, Charlotte," he said, pulling her toward Maya's bedroom. "I have just the suit in mind for you."

Putting on her best *fuck-you* smile, Charlotte followed him, but inside she was shaking like a leaf. *Please let it fit* was her silent prayer. A few minutes later she joined the guys on the deck and was rewarded for her years without fried food and ice cream. The aqua, floral two-piece was cut high on the bottom and showed off her long legs and toned stomach—*Thank you, Pilates!* But it was the top that had their eyes popping. Charlotte was right—her boobs would not be encased in a size six halter top, so while everything was covered, a lot of creamy, smooth cleavage was showing.

"Heaven help us" was the only comment from Noah, and Nick just looked at her as if his plan had backfired. Not waiting for another comment or for her courage to falter, Charlotte jumped into the warm Gulf of Mexico water and turned back to look at the two stunned men on the deck.

"Are we swimming or what?" She laughed and then turned and swam toward the pier.

Chapter 8

Then

Nick settled into the fifth grade and made friends with everyone, which was great for Lottie because now she was accepted as one of the class by everyone except, of course, Ashley and her group. Lottie didn't mind, though, because she still had Becca, and anyway, Lottie knew in her heart that Ashley was never going to be someone she wanted to be friends with.

At recess Lottie sometimes hung out with Becca and sometimes shot hoops with the other fifth graders, but after school she always walked home with Nick. Sometimes Noah and Becca walked with them, and sometimes they didn't, but it was Lottie's favorite part of the day regardless, even more than math!

"I don't have a dad," Lottie blurted out one afternoon a few weeks after meeting Nick. It was something she didn't usually talk about, but for some reason she knew Nick would understand.

"Did he die," Nick asked cautiously, "or are your parents divorced?"

As he spoke, Charlotte could feel the hurt in his voice. A few months later he would tell her about his parents, and the divorce that had broken his family apart, but for now he was totally focused on her.

"He died," sighed Lottie, "but it was way before I was born. He never even knew about me."

Reaching down to take her hand Nick smiled, and said, "You're pretty cool, I think your dad would have liked you a lot." Nick let go of her hand, but his words held on to her heart, and right then Lottie fell in love.

Chapter 9

Now

Nick and Noah met Charlotte at the pier, and for a moment they all just enjoyed a moment of peace in the late-afternoon sun. Charlotte spoke first. "So how long are you guys home for?" she asked.

Noah gave her one of his signature Hollywood-worthy smiles and replied, "I'm my own boss, so I can be here as long as you want me to, sweetheart." Charlotte lowered her head to hide her grin. She knew Noah was purposely goading his brother; she just wasn't sure why. Yes, Noah knew what had happened to end her friendship with Nick, but when she had seen him afterward, he had never mentioned it or taken sides. She was enjoying watching Nick squirm, but it was also kind of weird.

"Some of us have real jobs," Nick spat back, "but I have taken some vacation time, so much to your displeasure, *sweetheart*, you'll be seeing me around. Noah knows all about what's going on with Pop, and between the two of us we're going to find out why." With that Nick dived into the water and headed back to the marina. Noah rolled his eyes, and Charlotte laughed, but even after everything that had happened between them, she didn't like seeing Nick upset.

During the swim back to the marina Charlotte realized she had nothing to change into but her business suit and heels, and she groaned at the thought of putting her salty, sandy body back into her favorite outfit. She climbed up the ladder to the deck, and there was Nick freshly showered and dressed in board shorts and a T-shirt, and oh, if he didn't take her breath away. He helped her onto the deck, and if he was still mad, she couldn't tell.

"I laid a pair of sweatpants and a T-shirt on Maya's bed so you wouldn't have to get dressed up again," he said with a grin. "I know they'll be big on you, but I don't want you to ruin your fancy clothes."

Damn it! Why did he have to be so nice? It wasn't like she wanted to have a fight with him here, but it was hard to keep the shell closed around her heart when he acted so decent. Charlotte closed her eyes and remembered how she'd felt seeing Nick and Ashley together that night twelve years ago, hoping it would fuel the anger she needed for strength, but this time, instead of anger, it just brought back the hurt, and finding a quick escape was all she could think about.

Chapter 10

Then

The summer before seventh grade Lottie's body betrayed her, and while she had always been a little rounder than she liked, she now had boobs! Real boobs! It was like she wore an undershirt one day and woke up the next in a bra, and not a training bra, but one that had to give real support. Not only that but at her school physical she flunked the eye test and now had to have glasses. For two days she hid out in her house, not even seeing Nick when he came by, but by day three, her mom forced her out.

"Come on, Lottie," she said, pulling her daughter off the couch. "I need to take some beads to the Bird's Nest, and you're coming with me. A walk will make you feel better." Lottie loved her mom, but her mom didn't have a clue what life was like for her. To begin with, Maggie Luce was petite and voluptuous and beautiful with wavy, caramel hair and huge, green eyes, but she was also an unwed mother who lived like a gypsy or a hippie, Lottie wasn't sure which and totally did not understand that her lifestyle was frowned upon by most people in Anna Maria. Maggie had no problem bringing a man into her bed but had never allowed one into her heart since the night she'd become pregnant with Lottie at sixteen.

So on day three, Lottie and her mom headed out the back door to the Bird's Nest with Lottie praying that no one she knew would see them. Mom was talking business with the owner of the store, and without thinking Lottie stepped outside and ran right into Ashley and her BFF, Lea.

"OMG!" Ashley laughed. "What in the world happened to you?" She pointed to Lottie and laughed even louder. "Two of your eyes weren't enough; now you have four eyes—well, six, I guess, if you count the binoculars on your chest." Ashley and Lea continued to laugh, and as much as Lottie wanted to leave, she couldn't move a muscle. "Wonder what your buddy Nick will think of you now," Ashley said. As she walked away, she added, loud enough for Lottie to hear, "What a loser."

As soon as the girls were gone, Lottie ran home and spent the rest of the day crying and eating potato chips until her lips and tongue were swollen with salt. She had always known that Ashley didn't like her, but this was this first time Ashley had been really mean, and deep inside, Lottie knew it was just the beginning.

Chapter 11

Now

As soon as dinner was over, and the last plate was cleared, Charlotte said she had to go. Pop tried to get her to stay awhile and talk, but Charlotte was adamant. "I have a busy day tomorrow," she said, "but it was really great being here today, and I promise I won't wait so long to come back." *Just not when Nick is here,* she thought, but since he was just on vacation, that shouldn't be a problem.

After grabbing her clothes and the signed signature cards, she gave Pop a kiss on the cheek and thanked him again. She had almost made it to the door when she realized Nick was behind her. "I'll get your clothes washed and returned," she said, trying to get away without looking at him, but he followed her out the door.

"It really was great seeing you today," Nick said softly. "So many times I've thought about what it would be like to be here with you again—"

"Don't, Nick," Charlotte cut him off. "Please don't go there. I came here for your dad, and I'm glad that I did, but that's the only reason."

Nick nodded, but once again the dark hurt came over his eyes. He reached out and touched her cheek, smiled, and let her walk away. Again.

It had been a lot of years since Charlotte had really cried, but the minute she started her car, the tears began to fall, and pretty soon she felt as if she were in the middle of a monsoon. By the time she made it home, she was using her Prada blouse like a handkerchief, and she could feel the snot pooling in the back of her throat from all the sniffing. She was just about to shut the front door when her landline rang, and she tripped and fell over the desk. "Cwap!" She answered the phone in pain and said, still trying to keep all the yuck inside her nose, "Heddo."

"Charlotte?" came the familiar voice of her boyfriend, Peter. "Are you okay?"

Charlotte grabbed a tissue and put her head in her hands. Peter! She had forgotten all about Peter! They always talked on Monday evening before their standing date on Tuesday, but Nick had breezed into her office, and all thoughts of Peter had flown out the window.

"Peter, I'm so sorry," Charlotte explained. "I had this unexpected work thing come up, and it was kind of an emergency." She was stretching the truth, but for Peter work always came first, so she was hoping he would buy her excuse.

"As long as you're okay, I totally understand," he replied, which made Charlotte feel like shit. "I did call your cell a couple of times, though, and was surprised you didn't at least text back. Are you catching a cold? You sound a little nasally."

"I'm fine, Peter, truly. I think someone at my business thing has a cat, and you know how allergic I am. I'm sorry I caused you to worry, but it's been a really long day and I'm beat, so can we talk tomorrow?"

Charlotte had never lied to Peter and couldn't believe how easily she was doing it now, but she needed a big glass of wine, and she needed it now! That and a good night's sleep, and she'd be good as new.

"Okay," he replied without any hint that he wasn't buying her story. "I'll pick you up tomorrow at six thirty, and we'll go to Marni's. Good night."

Charlotte picked herself up from the floor, blew her nose, and groaned. Every Tuesday Peter picked her up at six thirty, and they went to Marni's. And every Monday he called to tell her that he'd pick her

26

up on Tuesday at six thirty and they'd go to Marni's. Every week the same thing. The same frigging call, the same frigging date! Couldn't they ever stay home and fry grouper and make homemade ice cream?

The blush started in her ears and worked its way down to her toes. *Where in the hell did that come from?* she thought. She filled the biggest glass she could find with her favorite Beach House wine and headed for the shower. *I'm covered with salt and sand and probably snot, so I'm going to drink this wine, take a hot shower, and get into my warm and comfortable bed, and when I wake up tomorrow, this day will all be a bad memory.*

Chapter 12

Now

Charlotte woke up on Tuesday morning to pouring-down rain, which was really unusual for the island in summer. Her eyes were puffy and swollen from crying, and she wanted nothing more than to go back to bed and call off sick, but of course her work ethic wouldn't allow that. After three cups of dark French roast coffee she was feeling better and started getting ready for work.

The stormy morning wasn't helping her mood. She grabbed a pair of navy-blue silk Halston trousers and a matching cashmere sweater, added a Lilly Pulitzer scarf for color, and picked out her lowest-heeled sandals, knowing that she wouldn't have time to change before dinner and that Peter didn't like it when she towered over him. At six feet Peter was tall by most standards, but put heels on Charlotte's five-foot-ten-inch frame, and she could easily be six foot one. She headed into the bathroom to see what kind of miracle her makeup could pull off but didn't feel very hopeful.

By seven twenty a.m. she was dressed and ready, looking once again like a market president. She lifted up her prayer to Gran, grabbed her umbrella, and ran out of her bungalow to her car. When she got to the bank, Carol and Dan, the bank's consumer lender, were deep in conversation, so she said "Good morning" and walked on by to her office. Needing some time to get focused on the day ahead, she shut her door and sat down, but the first thing she saw was the picture of her and Gran the day she'd graduated from Indiana University. Usually the picture brought her comfort and strength, but today it brought an onslaught of memories.

Chapter 13

Now

Lottie had been five the first time Gran had told her about her beginning in life. She had asked her mother lots of times why she didn't have a daddy, just a mommy and a grandma who lived far away, but her mother had never had a good answer. So one summer when they were visiting Gran in Indiana, Lottie had asked her.

Lottie had never forgotten how Gran had pulled her into her arms and told her, "I knew you were ours the moment I first saw you, and I've loved you every minute since. Your mommy loves you too, and those are the two most important things for you to remember."

Gran had told the story more like a fairytale the first few times, but by the time Charlotte had gotten to junior high, she'd known the truth. On the same day they'd met, her mother, at age sixteen, had slept with a college boy who was in Bradenton Beach on spring break, and Lottie was the outcome. The worst part was that Lottie's father had been killed in a car accident on his way back to Indiana a week later and had never even known about her. The best part was that, a few months after his death, when his mother finally found the courage to go through his things, she'd found a letter he had written to the girl who had so quickly captured his heart and, in her grief, reached out to the last person her son had found happiness with.

Charlotte picked up the picture and saw again how much she and Gran looked alike. They both were tall, with red hair and pale complexions, but Gran's eyes were brown, whereas Charlotte had the glass-green eyes of her mom. *How different would my life have been if Mom would have let Gran raise me when she offered?* She loved her mom, but her easygoing and easy-loving life had never been comfortable for Charlotte, and not for the first time Charlotte wondered if that was why she had such issues with relationships.

With a huge sigh she set the picture down and opened her computer. *I may not have this man thing all figured out, but I'm darn good at business!* she thought. Scrolling through her e-mails, she saw an address that had never been in her inbox before: ngreyson@gmail.com. Nick, Noah, Pop? There was only one way to find out. With a click of her mouse, the e-mail popped up in front of her: "We need to talk. Call me. Nick."

Shit, shit, shit! Who did he think he was to just waltz back into her life after twelve years and demand that she call him? Hitting the delete key, Charlotte swore out loud. *You can take your shiny badge and shove it up your firm, fine ass for all I care, special agent! I'm not one of the flunkies at your beck and call!* "Oh my gosh," she moaned. "Where did that thought even come from?" Charlotte slammed her fist on her desk and looked up to see her staff standing outside of her door with looks of shock on their faces. Taking a deep breath, Charlotte gave them her biggest smile and shooed them away as if they were children. This was not a good way to start her day.

Chapter 14

Now

Because she had gone to the marina instead of back to work on Monday afternoon, Charlotte had a lot of work to catch up on. She even opted for a quick yogurt and Diet Coke at her desk rather than taking a lunch break. By six o'clock, she was grumpy and ready to call it a day. The custodian, Bob, was the only one left in the building, so she told him she was leaving and headed to her car.

Thankfully the rain stopped by midmorning, but that left the air extra hot and muggy and her hair extra curly. Charlotte longed for a quick shower and change of clothes but had barely made it into her drive when Peter pulled up behind her. More than anything she wanted to open a bottle of wine, take Peter into her bedroom, and work off a little of the frustration she'd fought all day, but Peter did not do well with spontaneous, so she scrapped that thought and plastered a smile on her face.

"Are you doing casual days at the bank now?" Peter asked her first thing as he looked up and down at her pants and sweater. Charlotte bit her tongue, but it was all she could do to keep her irritation at bay. Peter had a theory that you needed to dress for the job you wanted and not the job you had, but he kept forgetting that she had the job she wanted! He was an up-and-coming attorney at a very good law firm, but his sights were set on making partner. He didn't leave the house in anything but a suit and tie, except on the weekends, and not always even then.

Deciding to just let it pass, Charlotte gave him a quick peck on the cheek and got into his light-blue BMW. "How was your day?" she asked brightly, although to be honest she knew she would be sorry. Peter had a habit of drawing out even the most mundane story to the point where she didn't listen, but it was better than discussing her work attire. By the time they arrived at the restaurant, Charlotte had calmed down, and Peter was just giving the final summation of his story.

The waitress came by with their menus, and Charlotte had just opened hers when Peter spoke up. "We'll each have a glass of your house chardonnay, and I'm starving, so let's go ahead and order." Having gone without lunch, Charlotte was all for that and was ready to tell the waitress what she wanted when Peter ordered for them. "We'll both have the lime grilled mahi-mahi, Caesar salad with dressing on the side, and the grilled asparagus."

Charlotte was not a happy camper. "Your choices sound delicious, Peter," she said guardedly, "but I was actually thinking about having steak tonight. I didn't have lunch, and I'm really hungry." She didn't want to fuss with him, because she knew he was very health conscious and understood her food issues, but she was not prepared for his response.

"You should have spoken up before the waitress left," he said. "But your eyes look a little puffy tonight, and since you wore pants to work today instead of a suit, I can only assume that you've been overindulging, particularly in the salt department, and I thought you would appreciate me helping you get back on track." Peter reached over and gave her hand a squeeze.

She had to force herself to stay calm. *Puffy eyes? Overindulging! Hadn't she told him last night about being around someone who had a cat? Yes, it was a lie, but he didn't know that! And she wore pants to work lots of times, just usually not on date nights.*

Charlotte sighed and looked over the table at Peter. He really was a very handsome man with his light-brown hair, dark-brown eyes, and wiry, muscular body that he kept in shape with healthy eating and lots of cycling. Even though he had a tendency to be a little overbearing from time to time, they had been together for over a year and had plans for a future. Well, at least Peter had a plan—make partner by thirty-three, get married at thirty-five, and have two children before age forty. Peter was successful and ambitious, and Charlotte knew she was lucky to have him, but right now she was hungry and horny, and not necessarily in that order. Seeing Nick again had her libido working overtime, so she decided to make her own plan, and that was to get Peter in her bed and Nick out of her head!

On Thursday nights Peter always stayed over after dinner, but Tuesdays were open for movies, drives through the upscale neighborhoods Peter wanted to live in someday, or sometimes even some adult activities. So as soon as they finished dinner and got back into Peter's car, Charlotte put her arms around Peter's neck and pulled him in for a long, hard kiss. Peter was a great kisser, and his response was just what she was hoping for. When they came up for air, Charlotte put her hand on Peter's thigh and smiled sheepishly. "My place?" was all she needed to say, and the BMW took off.

By the time they made it inside, Charlotte was practically panting and was looking forward to some down-and-dirty, hot sex. She and Peter had a nice love life, just nothing too adventurous, but she had always attributed the lack of real variation to her shyness where her body was concerned. Tonight though, she was on fire and ready for anything.

"There's a bottle of Beach House white in the fridge," Charlotte purred, giving Peter one more long, sultry kiss. "Get a couple of glasses, and I'll meet you in the bedroom."

Charlotte had been in St. Armands shopping the week before and had come across a wonderful lingerie store where she had treated herself to a few special items. One was a black lace teddy that she'd planned to save for a special occasion, which she decided tonight was. She threw off her work clothes and slipped the luxurious silk lace over her body, feeling cold and hot all at the same time. After a generous spritz of the Chloé perfume Peter had given her for Christmas, she ran her fingers through her thick, strawberry-blonde curls and turned and looked into the mirror.

The woman staring back looked sexy and filled with lust, so before she could talk herself out of leaving the bathroom, she opened the door and walked seductively into her bedroom. "Hey," she said in her most sultry voice, hoping that Peter would turn and look at her, "how about a glass of that wine?"

Peter was lying naked in her bed watching the news. She was looking forward to the biggest orgasm of her life, and he was watching the freaking news? She was an inch away from running out of the room or hitting him over the head with the wine bottle when he turned off the TV and looked at her. A huge smile appeared across his face, and it was enough for Charlotte to climb onto the bed, although all of a sudden, she was feeling way out of her comfort zone.

Peter pulled her into his arms and gave her another scorching-hot kiss and then moved his hands down to her very ample breasts. But instead of relieving the throb she felt with anything more than a quick squeeze, Peter asked, "How do you get this thing off?"

Get it off! Are you kidding me? Charlotte was screaming inside. *This little number cost me three hundred dollars, and you're ready for me to take it off?* Of course she didn't say that. Instead she slipped the straps seductively off her arms, hoping that Peter would at least feel aroused enough to want to pull it down over her hips, but nope, he just lay there.

This was way too much nakedness for a formerly fat girl, so Charlotte quickly pulled the sheet over herself and threw her beautiful teddy on the floor. At this point she was ready to chug the wine from the bottle and call it a day, but there was Peter with one of his smooth kisses again, and when he touched her between her legs, the simmer she felt there started into a full boil.

Charlotte reached for Peter, wanting to show him she was looking for the full experience tonight, but he took it as an invitation, and before she even knew what had happened, he was sheathed and headed for home. "Does that feel good?" he moaned as he entered her.

Charlotte decided he really wasn't expecting an answer, because a few thrusts later he was pounding away for dear life, and then it was over. Over! Her big night of unbridled sex, and it was over before she even got started. She wanted to scream and cry, but mostly she just wanted to get off, and to do that she was going to have to take matters into her own hands.

Peter lay on top of her for another minute before telling her how "amazing" that had been, and then he got up and headed for the bathroom. By the time he returned, Charlotte was dressed in sweatpants and a T-shirt, the ones Nick had loaned her the day before, and was watching David Letterman and gulping Beach House wine straight from the bottle.

"Charlotte," Peter both said and questioned, "are you okay? You're not acting like yourself."

What is myself? Charlotte wondered. *And is that even proper English?* At this point she had imbibed a lot of wine in a short amount of time, and her brain wasn't working too well. But she wanted Peter to leave, so she turned to him and gave him the out he was looking for. "I'm fine, Peter, just ready to fall asleep, so would you mind seeing yourself out?"

Peter gave her a soft kiss on her cheek and picked up his jacket from her chair. "Tomorrow is the weekly firm dinner meeting, but I'll call you on Thursday, okay? Tonight was great, by the way. I hope you enjoyed it as much as I did."

Charlotte nodded and laid her head down until she heard her front door close. As soon as she heard the BMW's engine start, she threw her pillow at her bedroom door and screamed. "What in the hell is happening to me?" she wailed. "A few days ago I was a strong, professional woman, and now I'm a hormonal mess! Damn you, Nick Greyson, you aren't going to do this to me again. I don't care how pretty you are or how my stomach dropped when I saw you without your shirt on or how I never really got over you; I am in control of my life."

Holy shit, did I just say I wasn't over Nick? It's been twelve years. How can that be? The bastard broke my heart and betrayed my trust. How can I feel anything for him but contempt?

Chapter 15

Now

Wednesday was a normal bright and beautiful day on the west coast of Florida, and Charlotte decided to use it to make some calls on prospective clients. There was talk of a new shopping area opening in Siesta Key, and Charlotte was itching to get the financing for the project. At her Rotary meeting on Monday one of the members had shared some information on the developer, and she was hoping to get the jump on the competition. Banking was a very competitive business, but Charlotte's mind for numbers always came in useful when she discussed options with clients. She was proud of the job she had done for Olde Florida. Her market was one of their most successful, and she intended to keep it that way. She took a quick look at her phone before heading out, and there was another e-mail from Nick. Once again the message was "We need to talk," but this time he'd added "please" before "call me." And once again, Charlotte deleted the message.

As she drove along listening to her favorite country radio station, all the songs played were about broken hearts or unrequited love, and that wasn't what she needed right now. Where were the songs about a strong woman kicking butt when she needed them!

She was just about to pass the marina when she realized just how much her anger with Nick had cost her the last twelve years. Monday with Pop and Noah had been great, and she vowed she wouldn't let her pride keep her away from them again. If it had been anyone but Ashley with him that night, would it have hurt so much and ended their friendship? Charlotte wasn't sure. But she knew the time had come to forgive, even if she couldn't forget, because otherwise how would she ever move on?

Chapter 16

Then

Eighth grade was like the preamble to adulthood in Lottie's mind, one year before high school and the three Ds. Dances, dating, and driving were the main topics of conversation between her and Becca, and they couldn't wait! Eighth grade was also the year that Ashley gave Lottie the nickname that would haunt and humiliate her every day of her life until she left for college.

Because of her mom's eclectic attitude about life, Lottie was always a little nervous when her mom decided to attend a function at school. She didn't want to feel embarrassed by her mom's '60s-style long skirts and peasant blouses or her free love philosophy, but junior high was hard enough without wondering if your mom had slept with one of your teachers or classmate's fathers. So on the day of the eighth-grade carnival, when Maggie announced she was helping in the kissing booth and needed Lottie to be the ticket taker, Lottie wanted to curl up and die! But, unlike most young girls, Lottie wasn't one to argue with her mom, and she agreed. Reluctantly.

The kissing booth was a huge success, and Lottie was even having a good time until Ashley walked by with Lea and a couple of boys from their class. "You know, Luce is an appropriate last name for Lottie's mom," Ashley said with spite, "because from what I hear she is..., loose I mean."

Ashley and Lea laughed, but one of the boys asked hopefully, "Do you suppose Lottie is too?"

Not really understanding what he was asking, Ashley scrunched up her nose and spit out, "Lottie's a loser." Then she smiled and said, "Lottie Loser, now there's an appropriate name." Ashley and her friends walked on but not before Ashley turned to make sure Lottie had heard them. She sent Lottie a snarky air-kiss, mouthed "Lottie Loser," and made an L with her right hand on her face, showing everyone in sight that she thought Lottie was a loser. Then she laughed and turned away. From that moment on Lottie's life wasn't the same.

Chapter 17

Now

Charlotte was beaming as she headed home from Siesta Key. She had a loan application in her briefcase and a verbal commitment from the developer of the shopping center to work exclusively with Olde Florida Bank. She knew that the bank's CEO, Martin Riggs, would be thrilled at the prospect, but then he was already a huge fan of Charlotte's. He was the person responsible for her market president title. Because of that, Charlotte always went the extra step when it came to bringing in business, and she loved a good win!

To celebrate, and because Peter had his firm thing that night, Charlotte decided to go home and order her favorite not-on-my-diet takeout, sesame chicken and vegetable fried rice. Mmm, she could almost taste the spicy sauce and crispy chicken just thinking about it. To offset some of the carbs, she changed into yoga pants and a tank top and worked on her elliptical machine until the food arrived.

Halfway through her feast she realized that she had ordered way more food than she could eat, so she packed it up and took it to her neighbor Mrs. Danvers. Mrs. D had been living in her bungalow by the beach for over fifty years, and at age ninety the only thing she had a problem with, as far as Charlotte knew, was her eyesight. That meant she'd had to give up driving and also that she was at the mercy of her daughter, Roma. Roma was as much a health nut as Peter was and wouldn't allow her mom anything that wasn't organic. Charlotte appreciated that Roma was concerned for her mother's health, but Mrs. D was ninety for heaven's sake. Hadn't she earned the right to eat what she wanted?

Charlotte knocked on the door and yelled out at the same time, "It's me, Mrs. D. I've brought you some contraband." The smile that greeted her when Mrs. Danvers opened the door was so sweet and so genuine it made Charlotte think of Gran. She knew her gran would have liked Mrs. D and would have definitely approved of Charlotte's friendship with her.

"Oh, Charlotte," Mrs. D giggled. "I could smell sesame chicken when you came up the walk. Come in, dear, and keep me company while I eat. Can I fix you a glass of iced tea?" Before she had become so dependent on Roma, Mrs. D would have fixed them both a glass of merlot, but Roma didn't think wine was an appropriate drink for someone her mother's age.

"That sounds perfect, Mrs. D," Charlotte replied, thinking what a shame it was that her friend's life was so controlled by a daughter she didn't see very often, but then she felt guilty when she realized how long it had been since she had spoken to or seen her own mother. *At least she's living her own life,* Charlotte thought and quickly gave all her attention back to Mrs. Danvers.

"How's that young man of yours?" Mrs. D asked between bites. "Am I ever going to hear wedding bells?"

Charlotte sighed and contemplated just how much she should share. Part of her thought she could talk to Mrs. D about her relationship with Peter, even the debacle of the previous night, but part of her was afraid talking about orgasms might just give Mrs. D a heart attack, so she went middle of the road. "I'm not really sure how to answer you," Charlotte replied honestly, "but don't be expecting wedding bells anytime soon. Peter is complicated to say the least."

"Is the sex good?" Mrs. Danvers asked as she scooped a bite of rice into her mouth.

Charlotte was so taken back that she snorted iced tea out of her nose before she calmed down enough to answer. "It's nice," she said, hoping that would be enough for a woman who had been widowed for twenty years, but Mrs. D surprised her.

"If he's not rocking your world now, honey, don't expect it to get any better. My husband, Leo, was great in bed, and he always believed in ladies first, if you get my drift." She gave Charlotte a knowing wink, and Charlotte just stared at her with her mouth agape. This ninety-year-old woman understood the magic that was lacking in her love life, and in that moment, she decided that she wasn't going to settle any longer. She was young and healthy and had a job she loved, and she was ready for a life that she loved to go with it.

As Charlotte walked back to her little house by the beach, the containers from the food safely in her hands so that Roma wouldn't find them in the trash, she vowed to make her own life plan, and that meant a visit to Becca's!

Chapter 18

Now

The afterglow of her successful day on Wednesday, combined with the spicy food and spicy conversation with Mrs. Danvers, had Charlotte in a great mood on Thursday. She knew that Peter would call her at one thirty to go over their dinner plans, just like he did every Thursday, but even that wasn't enough to put a damper on her day. She had made the decision that she and Peter were going to have a long-overdue conversation about their relationship and what they both wanted from it, and for the first time in a long time she felt as confident about her love life as she did her professional one.

As if reading her mind, the phone rang right at one thirty, and there was Peter. "Charlotte Luce," she answered with a smile when the direct line in her office rang.

"You sound perky this afternoon," Peter said. "Are you having a good day?"

Charlotte couldn't share any client or prospective-client information, so she just replied, "A very good day as a matter of fact."

Even when Peter said he'd pick her up at six thirty and they'd go to dinner at the Swordfish Grill, Charlotte's good mood hung on. They had dinner there every Thursday because it was peel-and-eat shrimp night, and six thirty was the time Peter always picked her up, but she refused to let it annoy her. Tonight Charlotte would calmly and rationally help Peter understand what she needed from their relationship. Hanging up the phone, she pictured the upcoming dinner, and how afterwards they could go back to her house and put her plan in action!

Not wanting another conversation with Peter about her attire, Charlotte had dressed carefully that morning in a Diane von Furstenberg wrap dress and low-heeled gladiator sandals. Her long curls were professionally secured in a tortoiseshell barrette, and she knew she looked good. Peter obviously agreed, because when he saw her, he smiled and said, "Very nice, Miss Luce." He then put his arm around her and gave her a soft kiss, and Charlotte was feeling very confident about the evening and their future.

At the restaurant Charlotte's courage started to wane, so when Peter asked her if she'd like a glass of wine, she shook her head and asked the waitress to bring her a lemon drop. Raising an eyebrow, Peter asked, "A lemon drop, Charlotte, are you sure? All that sugar and strong alcohol just doesn't seem like the right choice for you."

Taking a deep breath, Charlotte looked at the waitress instead of at Peter and repeated her request. When she looked back at Peter, she could tell he wasn't pleased, but thankfully he let the matter drop. "Any exciting new cases?" Charlotte asked him, hoping to get the evening back on track.

"Another girlfriend of a professional athlete is claiming abuse, but I'm not sure where it will go. Ever since we won that big settlement for Misty Compton, we've had more than our share of requests, but I don't think that's the reputation the firm is wanting to capitalize on."

Charlotte nodded, aware that she didn't know enough about the situation to make a comment, although she never liked it when she heard a woman was being abused. She knew all relationships had issues, but she would never stay with a man who was abusive, physically or mentally.

The waitress brought their drinks, and Charlotte drank a long draw of the tangy, sweet citrus concoction in her glass. "Yum," she purred, "this is so good." Peter gave her another questioning glance and asked if she was ready to order.

When the waitress returned, Charlotte said with a smile, "I'll have the shrimp pasta, house salad with the sweet-onion dressing on the side, and another one of these." She pointed to her now-empty martini glass.

"Charlotte," Peter scolded, "maybe you should rethink that. All that starch and sugar will just make you feel sluggish, and, well, you know, it's Thursday. I was thinking we would share the steamed shrimp and a spinach salad."

By now the vodka and lemon liqueur were making Charlotte's insides feel warm, but that was nothing compared to the heat that was rising up her face. Her itinerary for the evening was definitely getting off track, and she needed to find a way to get it back. "I know what I want, Peter, and I know what I need, so please, let's enjoy our dinner, and we can discuss the days of the week later."

The poor waitress started to write down Charlotte's order, but Peter wouldn't let it go. "Charlotte, we always get the steamed shrimp on Thursday, but if you'd prefer a different kind of salad, I can be flexible."

Flexible! she screamed internally. Peter was about as flexible as a piece of lead pipe, especially where food was concerned. "Please bring me another drink while we look at the menu again," Charlotte told the waitress, with a little more strength than she meant to. The poor girl almost ran in her delight to be done with them, a feeling Charlotte was beginning to relate to. At this point she knew for a fact that the conversation she had hoped to have with Peter was never going to happen, and as she looked into his handsome face, she knew she had to get out of there, but how? Thankfully he made it easy for her.

"What's going on with you tonight?" Peter asked, and then he threw in the clincher. "Is it that time of the month?"

Without even thinking Charlotte hissed, "What the fuck, Peter?" Peter gasped and turned a whiter shade of pale. For Peter, vulgarity, especially in a woman, rated right up there with desecrating the flag, but Charlotte knew it was the only thing to shut him up. After downing the new drink that had magically arrived at the table, Charlotte stood up and with heat in her voice said, "Take me home. Now!"

46

The ride home was painfully silent but thankfully short, as Charlotte lived only a few miles from the restaurant. When they pulled into her driveway, she bolted out of the car while Peter took the time to grab his overnight bag. "You aren't going to need that," Charlotte spit out as she unlocked the front door, paying no attention as Peter continued up the walk.

"This isn't working anymore, Peter," she said forcefully. "You need to just go home and give me some time to think."

"Think about what?" he asked. "A week ago everything was great, and two nights ago you were all over me, and now you say this isn't working? If that isn't hormones talking, I don't know what is."

Charlotte was fuming. *All over him? Hormones? I'll show him hormones!* she decided. "Tell me, Peter," she asked as calmly as possible, "what do you want from this relationship, and where do you see it heading?"

Peter gave a sigh of relief. "Is that what this is about, Charlotte? You want a commitment from me? I thought you understood my plan and agreed with it. You know how important it is to me to make partner before we even discuss marriage, and that's probably two years down the road."

Unfricking believable, she thought. *He doesn't have a clue.* "What about my life plan, Peter? Have you ever given any thought to that? Because I know what I want, and I'm not waiting for it any longer."

"Charlotte, be reasonable," he pleaded. "We aren't ready to talk about marriage, but we have a good thing, and you know I'm devoted to you." He reached out to pull her into a hug, but she backed away.

This time she couldn't keep the anger and the hurt out of her voice and ended up responding a little louder than she intended. "If you think this is about getting married, you're crazy! This is about me taking control of my life for a change and getting what I want." Peter opened his mouth to respond, but Charlotte cut him off. "I need a man who will respect my decisions and who wants my input on our life. I want passion, Peter; I want to be so hot that I'm ready to combust. I want to feel sexy and desired and loved, and I'm not waiting any longer for

47

those feelings. We're not on the same page, Peter, so let's end this now before it gets any harder."

Before Peter could say another word, there was a knock on the screen door, and Charlotte looked up to see Nick standing in her doorway. "Is this a bad time?" he asked sheepishly.

Holy, holy shit! Charlotte thought. How long had Nick been standing there, and how much had he heard? Charlotte looked from Nick, who had a huge smile on his face, to Peter, who was as angry as she'd ever seen him, and closed her eyes, hoping when she opened them they'd both be gone, but of course she wasn't that lucky.

"What are you doing here, Nick?" she asked sarcastically.

"You didn't respond to my emails, so I decided if you weren't interested in talking by phone, we'd talk in person," he answered.

Charlotte was certain she saw smoke coming out of Peter's ears. "It's all starting to make sense now," he growled. "The infamous Nick comes back to town, and nothing else matters. I thought you got over your schoolgirl crush a long time ago, Charlotte, but obviously all it takes is one of his big hero looks, and you're ready to throw away what we have to finally get him into your bed."

Charlotte was mortified, but the expression on Nick's face was one of amusement, even though he was trying to act serious and offended. "Get. Out. Now," Charlotte spat at Peter. "This conversation is over."

Peter grabbed his bag and gave one more parting shot before walking out the door. "I offered you stability and an adult relationship, Charlotte. I've never cheated on you and would never have hurt you the way he did. Think about that while you're taking your trip down memory lane." And with that he slammed the door and left.

Chapter 19

Then

During the summers between their years in high school, Nick, Noah, Lottie, and sometimes Becca would work at the marina selling bait to the local fishermen or working in the store or snack bar while Pop and Maya took care of the commercial fishing boats. It was an easy job that allowed Lottie to be away from home and with her good friends. It was the best of both worlds for Lottie, especially now that her mom had started talking about joining a commune once Lottie graduated. From the way her mom talked about it, Lottie was pretty sure it was more like a nudist colony or sex commune than a place to grow vegetables, but she never had the guts to come right out and ask.

The downside to them spending so much time together was the nights when Nick and Noah would go off on their own or with a group of guys from school. Lottie knew Nick loved her, but only as a friend or a sister, and her worst fear was that on those guys' nights they were meeting up with girls. By the time he was a sophomore, Noah already had a reputation for being a player, and Lottie was scared he would lead Nick down that path too. The four of them talked about almost everything, but given her mother's history, sex was definitely not a topic Lottie was comfortable discussing, not even with Becca, who had recently decided she was going to become a nun!

When Lottie was sixteen and ready to head into her senior year, Gran sent her a ticket to fly to Indiana for the month of June. Lottie was thrilled to spend that much time with her grandmother but uncertain about leaving her mom alone and being away from Nick for a whole month. Pop promised to check in on Maggie every week to make sure she was okay, and Becca promised to be Lottie's eyes and ears where Nick was concerned, so with excitement and fear Lottie boarded the airplane and stepped into another world.

Lottie wasn't Gran's only grandchild, but they had a special bond because Lottie was Gran's last link to her son. Gran didn't treat Lottie any differently than her other grandchildren, but she did do her best to spoil her when she could. So, during Lottie's month in Indiana she helped Lottie move from being a girl to being a young woman.

With a trip to the optometrist, Lottie's hated glasses were replaced by contacts. A visit to a fancy salon showed Lottie how to work with her naturally curly hair and toned down the red to a beautiful strawberry blonde. Lottie was thrilled with the results and even decided to work on her excess pounds by taking daily walks around Gran's farm. By the time July rolled around and Lottie's time with Gran was coming to an end, she felt like a new person.

"I'll never be able to thank you for this summer," Lottie said to Gran as she held back the tears. "I love you, Gran. You know that, don't you?"

"Oh, my Lottie, you don't have to thank me for anything, and of course I know that you love me. Your dad would have been so proud of the beautiful person you are, inside and out, and you are like the daughter I never had." Gran hugged the girl that would soon be a woman and put her on the plane for home.

If Lottie thought leaving was scary, coming back was even harder. The thoughts of all the things that could have happened during the month kept running through her brain like a broken movie reel, but Becca had assured her that everything was fine at the marina and Lottie had been in contact with her mother, so she had to put such thoughts out of her mind. To be honest, her biggest fear was coming home and finding that Nick had a girlfriend, but that was a fear she had even when they were together. She couldn't wait to see him and show off her new look. Maybe now he would see her like she saw him.

Maggie was deep into making jewelry on the day Lottie was due home, so Nick and Noah agreed to pick her up at the airport. She was so nervous that she stumbled getting off of the plane, which only added to the sweat she was feeling from head to toe. But when she looked up and saw Nick and Noah standing there with huge smiles on their faces, she couldn't think of anything but how much she had missed them and how good it was to be home.

"Look at you, Shortcake!" Noah exclaimed, pulling her in for a hug. "No more glasses covering your pretty green eyes, and it looks like I'm going to need to find a new name for you." Noah had started calling her Strawberry Shortcake because of her red hair soon after they had met, but unlike Ashley's nickname, Lottie knew this one had been made with love.

Lottie did a little turn to give the guys the full effect and then looked at Nick. She had missed him and hoped more than anything he was still the friend she had left. When he reached out for her hand and said quietly, "It's great to have you home, Lottie," she knew everything was going to be okay.

Chapter 20

Now

Charlotte reached up and grabbed her locket, needing wisdom from her gran. She wasn't someone who really argued, yet she'd stood up to Peter. She wasn't someone who yelled, but she'd done that too. But what worried her the most wasn't what she'd said or done to Peter but what Nick had overheard and what was going on in his head. She knew they needed to talk, but right now she was vulnerable, hungry, and a little fuzzy from too much vodka.

Realizing that she needed time to get her head on straight, she grabbed her purse and announced to Nick, "I promise I'll call you in a few days, but I'm starving, and I've had a couple of drinks, so I'm going to walk over to the Crab Shack for some dinner and a beer." She locked her front door and started heading toward the beach. When she realized Nick was following right beside her, she pleaded, "Go home, Nick. I need some time alone."

"Funny thing, but Noah and I made plans to meet at the Crab Shack tonight after you and I talked, so I'll just walk along with you. I can pick up my car later."

Charlotte groaned but didn't have any more fight left in her. She decided to pretend that Nick wasn't walking so closely beside her and that he didn't smell incredible or look like sex on a stick, and maybe when she got to the bar, he'd go away! Fat chance. They had no sooner walked in the door than Noah greeted them and called them over to the booth he was sitting in. "Karaoke tonight," Noah exclaimed. "Good thing I got here when I did, because this was the last booth."

Charlotte wanted to turn and run, but the vodka was really sloshing in her stomach and she knew she needed food. Reluctantly she sat down and looked straight into the blue eyes of her biggest nightmare. She leaned her elbows on the table and put her head in her hands. "Shit, shit, shit," she mumbled and realized both Nick and Noah had heard her.

"Let's get you a drink and some food, Shortcake," Noah teased. "You look like you've had a long day."

After a plate of crab cakes and three Blue Moons, Charlotte was feeling no pain, and when the crowd took a break from karaoke and someone dropped some coins in the jukebox, Charlotte grabbed Noah's hand and pulled him onto the dance floor. Noah was a reputed ladies' man and knew his way around the dance floor, but Charlotte wasn't prepared for him to pull her tightly into his body and wrap his hands around her back. Way down on her back. Charlotte felt the heat rise on her face, but it felt so good to be held that she didn't pull away. When the first song ended and another one started, Noah held on, slipping his hands a little lower and whispering in her ear, "You know this is driving my big brother wild, right? He's over there scowling and stripping the label off his beer bottle, probably wishing it was you." Noah chuckled and turned Charlotte so she could get a good look at Nick, and sure enough he looked pissed! Charlotte had never been a tease and had no real clue how to flirt, but with courage from the alcohol, she ground her hips into Noah and smiled sweetly at Nick.

"Whoa there, Shortcake," Noah moaned as Charlotte realized she was rubbing up against a very large erection. "I'm only human," he said with a smile. More embarrassed than she thought possible, she pulled back.

Needing to cool down and stop the pounding in her heart, Charlotte headed to their booth and ordered another beer. She took a long swig and looked at Nick through her lashes but couldn't get a read on his expression. She knew he was angry, but she wasn't sure why. Did it bother him that she was dancing with Noah, or was there something else going on? The beer was about to give her the courage to ask when instead she said, "I think I'm going to pass out."

Before she could slide off the bench and onto the floor, Nick had her in his arms and was yelling at Noah, "Grab her things and come on before our lady banker really embarrasses herself."

In fewer than five minutes they were helping Charlotte inside her house. At some point during the short ride Charlotte began to giggle and talk a little incoherently, but they were no sooner in the door than her ramblings became very apparent. She pulled the tie on her wrap dress and started to slip it off her shoulders. Before Nick could stop her, both men got a good look at her large breasts tucked inside a sheer white lace bra and matching panties that allowed them a spectacular view of her dark-red curls.

Noah shook his head and grinned. "I guess Shortcake is still appropriate," he chuckled while his brother shot daggers his way.

"I've got this, Noah," Nick said in a very controlled FBI kind of voice. "You can go."

Noah gave his brother a short salute but continued laughing as he headed out the door. "There's a tiger in that tank, big brother. I hope you've got your gun well oiled."

Chapter 21

Then

Senior year seemed to go by in a flash, and before Lottie knew it, graduation was upon them. Nick had been asked to join the swim team at Florida State, so a lot of his time was spent at practice and at meets. Lottie had attended as many of his meets as she could because she knew that once they left for college, nothing would ever be the same. Her math abilities had earned her a perfect score on the math portion of her SATs, so she would be heading to Indiana University in the fall on a full-ride academic scholarship.

Gran had flown down for her graduation ceremony but could only be away from the farm for a few days. As much as Lottie hated to see Gran leave, she knew that come September they would be seeing more of each other since the drive from Martinsville to Bloomington was such a short one. Lottie and her mom took Gran back to the airport, and after a few tears and a big hug, Gran was off.

"Lottie," her mom said on the drive back to Anna Maria, "I've been honest with you about my plans to leave the island after your graduation, right? I won't leave until you're safely at IU, but I am going to go."

Lottie looked at her mom and for the first time had the courage to ask a question she had wondered about her whole life. "Why didn't you ever get married, Mom?" she asked. "I know it isn't because you didn't have the opportunity."

Charlotte could see the smile in her mother's eyes as she spoke. "I knew I loved your dad the moment I laid eyes on him," she said softly, "and I know he loved me. There was never another man who even came close to giving me that feeling, although you and I both know I never stopped looking for it. Sex is a physical release that human beings need, but sex with love is magic, and I only found that magic with one man. I know I haven't been the mother you've wanted, Lottie, but don't ever doubt how much I love you. You've had your gran and Mr. Greyson and Nick to give you the structure that you've needed, but I was here to give you life."

Lottie didn't know how to respond, so she reached over and gave her mom's hand a squeeze. She couldn't imagine what it would be like to have a baby at her age, especially one she had to raise alone. She knew her mom's parents had disowned her when they'd found out she was pregnant. Maybe Lottie hadn't been fair to her mother all these years, thinking she was flighty and ungrounded, and even if she was, what difference did it make? Her mom was right; Lottie had love and she had structure, and even if she did have a nemesis in Ashley, her life was pretty good.

Chapter 22

Now

Charlotte's internal alarm went off at five o'clock every morning, and despite her horrific headache, Friday was no exception. For a few moments she felt disoriented and couldn't remember even going to bed. Pretty quickly she realized that instead of the IU sleep shirt she wore most nights when she slept alone she still had on her bra and panties, which she never slept in. Afraid of what she might find, she gingerly let her fingers creep to the other side of the bed and heaved a huge sigh of relief when she found it empty. But was there someone in her house? Snippets of Peter and Nick and Noah were trying to work their way from a bad dream to a reality, so she quietly slipped on her robe and stepped out of her bedroom. She checked every room of her small bungalow and found them all empty. Just to be on the safe side, she checked the lanai and garage as well, but they were empty too. Breathing a little easier, she locked all the doors and headed back to the kitchen for some coffee. Some strong coffee.

"I've got to cut back on alcohol," Charlotte groaned as she popped three aspirin in her mouth and her favorite K-Cup into her Keurig. Emeril's Extra- Bold, Extra- Dark roast was just what she needed on a morning like this, and she was thankful for how quickly she had the steaming mug of fortitude in her hands. Taking a big sip, she headed to the shower, trying to figure out how she was going to salvage the week that had pretty much gone to hell.

Fridays really were casual days at Olde Florida Bank. In fact, they were dress-down-for-charity days, an idea of Charlotte's that she was proud had caught on with the entire company. For a donation to the designated charity of the month employees were allowed to wear denim jeans, or skirts, with bank-logo shirts to work, and this Friday, more than most Charlotte was thrilled to be able to dress comfortably for the day. She slipped into her favorite pair of Silver Jeans and a white Olde Florida polo shirt, pulled her curls into a ponytail, put on a little mascara and lip gloss, and decided she looked as good as possible under the circumstances.

As usual Charlotte arrived at the bank at seven thirty, and Carol and Dan were already there working. She felt like she hadn't been very engaged with her staff all week, so despite the throbbing behind her eyes, she took a minute to talk with them about their weekend plans. She valued all her staff, but Carol and Dan had been with the bank when Charlotte had been hired, and she knew how important they were not only to customers but also to the rest of the team. After a few minutes of small talk, she excused herself and headed to the solitude of her office.

At nine Carol unlocked the lobby doors, and the first person in headed directly to Charlotte's office. "Uh, Miss Luce," said Andy Morris, the pharmacy technician from the drugstore across the street, "I have a delivery for you."

Charlotte stood up, looking very confused as Andy handed her a beautiful, shiny red gift bag. "I didn't know you made deliveries, Andy," Charlotte said. "What's going on?"

"The manager didn't think it made sense to say no to the FBI," Andy said. "And besides, have you seen how big that guy is? I wouldn't want to be on his bad side."

Nick! Charlotte thought, and her right eye started to twitch. As the morning had worn on, she had started to remember the events of the night before, and they all circled back to Nick. But when she opened the bag, she had a hard time holding back her smile. Inside was a cold liter of 7 Up, a bottle of aspirin, and a package of Lance peanut butter cheese crackers. The crackers had been her favorite snack when they'd worked at the marina as kids, and Charlotte couldn't believe Nick had remembered.

At the bottom of the bag was a note in Nick's handwriting. As she read it, her smile was quickly replaced by a frown. "We're still going to have that talk, Shortcake, but I'm going to give you the day off for bad behavior. Drink lots of fluids, eat foods that will be easy on your stomach, take the aspirin as needed, and I'll call you tomorrow. I hope you slept well. The 'infamous' Nick."

Her face bright red, Charlotte fumbled in her purse to find Andy a tip.

"It's all been taken care of, Miss Luce," he mumbled. "I was just told to bring you the bag and make sure you opened it." With that he turned and left.

Charlotte sat down and put her head in her hands. "Shortcake," she whispered to herself. Noah was the only person who had ever called her Shortcake. Having Nick say it meant that standing in her underwear in front of him and Noah the night before had really happened and wasn't the dream she had been praying it was; it was an actual nightmare.

On Fridays Charlotte usually bought her staff lunch to show her appreciation for their hard work during the week, and this Friday everyone wanted pizza. Charlotte was happy to treat them to whatever they wanted, but today the smell of the garlic and the sausage was about to make her throw up, and it made her head throb worse. She knew she needed to spend some time in the break room while people ate, though, so she popped three more aspirin, grabbed one of her peanut butter crackers and her 7 Up, and did her best to be one of the team.

The pain in her head was just starting to subside when Pam, the customer service representative, came into the break room carrying a huge bouquet of red roses. "You were either awfully good or awfully bad last night," Pam teased as she handed Charlotte the vase. The smell of the roses, combined with the smell of the pizza, was too much for Charlotte, and she covered her mouth and ran to the bathroom. After

59

emptying her stomach, she looked in the mirror and decided she knew what she would look like when she died. The mascara she had put on that morning was running down her face, and her lips were dry and cracked. She wanted nothing more than to curl into a ball and cry, but she knew that she had to pull herself together. Besides, crying would make her head hurt worse.

Picking herself off the bathroom floor, she washed off her face and did the only professional thing she could think of. She lied. "Carol," Charlotte called to her assistant, "I think I must have a touch of food poisoning, so I'm going home for the rest of the day." She put the vase of roses in the lobby for everyone to enjoy, grabbed the card that was attached and her purse, and was out the door before anyone could ask questions. Sometimes it was good to be the boss.

When she got home, Charlotte kicked off her TOMS and crawled into bed, not even bothering to take off her clothes. She woke up shortly after seven. Her headache was gone, and her stomach was no longer turned inside out. Deciding that a shower, a bowl of soup, and an *I Love Lucy* marathon sounded like the best evening she'd had all week, Charlotte climbed out of bed and stripped off her rumpled clothes. She was just about to throw her jeans in the hamper when she saw the card from the roses peeking out of the back pocket.

She knew the roses were from Peter, and as much as she didn't want to read the card, she felt she owed him that much. Could it say anything to change her mind? Did she even want it to? She cautiously removed the card from the envelope and sighed, realizing quickly that Peter just didn't have a clue. Typed on the card from the florist were the words "This is my big cycling weekend in Tampa. I'll call you on Monday evening. Love, Peter."

Charlotte shook her head and threw the card in the trash. In typical Peter fashion he thought he could ignore the problem away, but Charlotte was done with swallowing her feelings. She had known all along that she wasn't really in love with Peter, and she knew now that she wasn't going to settle for anything less in her future. Mrs. D had found her true love, and to be honest, so had Charlotte's mom. For the first time since Nick, Charlotte was willing to go in search of her own.

Chapter 23

Then

The summer after graduation was going by in a blur, but it was the best one of Lottie's life. She spent the days working or hanging out with her friends at the marina, swimming in the warm waters of the Gulf of Mexico, or playing volleyball on the beach. Nights meant trolley rides to Two Scoops for ice cream, moonlight walks on the beach, and just Nick. Noah was making it his mission to sleep with every recently graduated girl from Bradenton High School so he took off shortly after dark every evening. Becca's devotion to the church had her involved in something almost every night, but secretly Lottie was fine with that. She and Nick talked a lot on those evenings about college, what their goals were, and what they wanted out of life, but they never talked about how college was going to change them and their relationship. Lottie thought about it a lot but never said anything, as the summer was just too wonderful. Besides, if she tried hard enough, she could pretend she and Nick were a real couple, and she didn't want to risk that for anything.

So, when Nick took her hand one evening in August and asked her to meet him at eight o'clock at the pool house during the traditional summer send-off for seniors, Lottie was sure he had something important to say to her about their future, and her heart told her it was something good.

Chapter 24

Now

Despite her hangover on Friday Charlotte was still up at five on Saturday morning and ready to start her day. She put on a pair of hot-pink running shorts and matching sports bra; threw her hair up in a messy bun; slipped into her favorite Nike running shoes; grabbed her phone, keys, and a bottle of water; and stepped out into the peaceful cerulean-blue Florida morning. With her windows rolled down to take advantage of the breeze before the humidity set in, she let out a sigh that she felt had been building up all week.

The Bradenton Botanical Gardens was a hidden gem as far as Charlotte was concerned and a wonderful place to run. The smell of the tropical flowers was amazing, and the beautiful colors and arrangements energized her. She locked her car, put her phone and keys in the zip pocket of her shorts, and did a few warm-up stretches before starting out. She went about two miles and was just working up a good sweat when she heard footsteps coming up behind her.

Charlotte had never been one to panic easily, but she'd been running at the gardens on Saturdays mornings at this time for a couple of years now and had never so much as seen another person. And from the sounds behind her this person was big. She reached for the zipper on her shorts and was just about to pull out her phone when a voice called out to her. "Well, Charlotte Luce, what are you doing out running at the crack of dawn on a Saturday morning?"

She knew that voice, so very coyly she turned and replied, "It's how I stay… all grown up."

The sun was just beginning to come up, but Charlotte could clearly see the amusement on Nick's face. She could also see that he was staring a little too hard at her sweat-soaked sports bra, but she wasn't about to give him any satisfaction by trying to cover her chest. Instead she put her hands on her hips and stared back, and crap if that wasn't the wrong thing to do! She could feel her nipples start to pebble just looking at Nick's finely sculpted body, and the minute she saw the smirk on his face, she knew she'd been had.

"Mind if I run with you?" Nick asked as Charlotte started moving on.

"It's a free country," she hissed as she picked up speed, sounding more like she was twelve than twenty-nine.

"Come on, Lottie, give me a break!" Nick called out. "I'm really trying here, and I don't know what else to do."

Charlotte slowed down to let him catch up because she did know he was trying, and she was tired of fighting him. She gave a little wave behind her back, and within a second he was next to her and they were running side by side.

The trip around the gardens was eight miles total, but all too quickly they were back at the parking lot. It had been nice running with Nick, but now Charlotte felt awkward and didn't quite know how to say good-bye. She was reaching for her keys when Nick spoke.

"Have dinner with me tonight, Charlotte," he said. "You owe me a talk, and I really want to spend some time with you when you're not flirting with my brother or drinking to excess." Nick ran his hands through his hair. "Shit, that did not come out right."

Seeing the agony on his face, Charlotte started to laugh, and pretty soon Nick was laughing with her. "You really know how to make a girl feel special, Special Agent," she teased, "but as tempting as that offer is, I'm headed to New Smyrna Beach to spend the rest of the weekend with Becca and her kids. Her husband's at a conference in Miami, so we have some girl time planned."

"Becca?" Nick asked. "You mean our Becca?"

"Yes, our Becca," replied Charlotte. "Did you forget about her?"

Nick just shook his head. "I didn't forget about her, but I never expected Sister Rebecca Rose to give it up to a mere mortal."

"Oh, not a mere mortal," Charlotte purred "Jared is a pediatrician who works with Doctors Without Borders, and he's *hot*! Really *hot*! And he must know what he's doing, because they have three and a third kids and can't keep their hands off each other." Nick growled, and Charlotte giggled. It felt good, really good.

"How about Tuesday then?" he asked. "I have to go back to Tampa on Monday, but I'd love to take you to the Anna Maria Pier at sunset and take a walk on the beach. Please, Charlotte, just say yes."

"Okay, Nick." She smiled. "Yes. Tuesday it is. And thanks for the care package yesterday. It meant a lot." And with that she got in her car and drove away.

The drive to New Smyrna took about three hours, so Charlotte liked to stop midway and treat herself to a Mocha Frappuccino at Starbucks. It was one of her secret indulgences. Oh, the frosty decadence tasted good, especially on a hot summer day. With the radio up and a little whipped cream on her lip, Charlotte couldn't help but smile. She was finally moving forward with her life, and a visit with Becca was just the finishing touch that she needed.

Chapter 25

Now

"Aunt TT's here! Aunt TT's here!" the three Tyler children shouted as they opened the door and grabbed Charlotte's legs all at the same time. Charlotte kneeled down to their level and wrapped her arms around the three towheads she loved so much. A tiny ache in her heart reminded her how much she wanted a family of her own, but until that time, she had Becca's babies to spoil rotten.

"Let me get a good look at you, guys." She laughed. "I swear you've grown a foot since the last time I saw you!" Taking her namesake, two-year-old Lolly, into her arms, Charlotte ruffled the hair of five-year-old JD and then curtsied to the princess of the family, four-year-old Anna.

"Princess Anna Banana," Charlotte said with as much dignity as she could muster, "may I enter the palace?"

Anna giggled her assent and touched Charlotte's shoulder with a plastic scepter. "You may enter, Queen Lottie Lou," she replied. Then, forgetting her royal manners, she wrapped herself around Charlotte, and the four of them fell to the ground in a sea of giggles.

"Okay, Tyler Tykes," came a voice of authority. "Auntie Charlotte is my playdate, so give your momma some room." In awe the children stepped back and watched as their mom and Aunt Lottie hugged and cried.

"It happens every time," JD said with a shake of his head. Smiling, he yelled to his sisters, "Bet you can't catch me," and the three ran off giggling, leaving Charlotte and Becca to themselves.

"I'm just working on lunch for my heathens," Becca said, slipping her arm around Charlotte's waist. "Come sit in the kitchen with me and tell me absolutely everything!"

"Well," started Charlotte, "I'm pretty certain that I broke up with Peter and—"

"Pooh on Peter," Becca retorted, bunching up her nose. "You should have dumped his sorry ass months ago. Now tell me about Nick."

"There isn't a lot to tell really. He's back in town to help his dad and—"

"Is he still so gorgeous? Have you kissed him yet? Have you slept with him yet? Are you still in love with him? Come on, Lottie, I'm the pregnant mother of three; I want to live vicariously through you, so give me the dirt!"

Charlotte was dumbstruck. "First of all," she replied cautiously, "why didn't you ever tell me that you didn't like Peter? Secondly, Nick has only been home a few days, and except for when I stripped down to my undies in front of him and Noah, everything has been very aboveboard. And third, you probably have more sex in a week than I've had in my lifetime, so living vicariously through me is going to be pretty much like your summer living with the nuns at Saint Aggies."

"You stripped in front of Nick *and* Noah? Now we're getting somewhere," Becca shot back with a smile.

Putting her head in her hands, Charlotte groaned. "I promised myself I'd cut back on alcohol, but do you have any wine? I know you're preggers and all, but I could really use a big glass right now."

Becca just shook her head and ushered Charlotte into the kitchen. After a kid-friendly lunch of peanut-butter-and-jelly sandwiches, sliced apples, and grapes, it was time for the kids to rest and for Charlotte and Becca to really talk.

"Okay, girlfriend, we have iced tea, organic orange juice, or mineral water with lime. What's your pleasure?"

Charlotte groaned. "When did you quit serving adult beverages to your guests?"

Becca pointed to her belly bump and laughed. "Remember the last time you came for a visit and baby Charlotte had finally given up nursing? You and I decided to celebrate me being allowed to drink alcohol again by making a pitcher of mango mojitos. That pitcher resulted in us getting a little tipsy, so like a good daddy Jared took the kids over to visit Grandma, and I made another pitcher of drinks. Long story short, you fell asleep somewhere in the middle of pitcher number two, and as soon as Jared brought the kids home and we put them to bed, I jumped his bones, and you're looking at the result. You can still have coffee in the morning, though, so suck it up, buttercup!"

Charlotte couldn't help but laugh. "You would have jumped his bones if we'd only been drinking soda, so don't try to lay a guilt trip on me. And suck it up, buttercup? I've missed you so much, Becca, especially your way with words!"

Becca gave her friend's hand a quick squeeze, and then her tone became more serious. "We've been friends since kindergarten, Lottie, and there isn't anything I wouldn't do for you. I'm going to get you a big glass of cold iced tea, and we're going to sit on the deck, and you're going to tell me all about what's going on."

Chapter 26

Then

Lottie was so nervous the day of the senior send-off that she couldn't think of anything but what Nick wanted to talk with her about. Was he finally going to tell her that he liked her as more than a friend? Was he going to ask her to be his girlfriend? Was he going to kiss her? The suspense was killing her, and she wanted nothing more than to be able to talk with Becca, but the send-off was sponsored by the incoming senior class, which meant Becca was spending the day setting up and decorating. Normally the fact that they were in different grades wasn't a problem, but today Lottie needed her friend. *At least she'll be at the party tonight,* she told herself, knowing that she would want to tell Becca about her conversation with Nick as soon as possible.

Lottie had never been one for primping, but she wanted so much to look perfect for tonight that she spent the biggest part of the afternoon getting ready. Her mom helped with her naturally curly hair so that it hung in waves around her shoulders, and she even put on mascara and lip gloss, something she normally shied away from. With some of her graduation money from Gran she'd splurged on a navy-blue, polka-dot one-piece bathing suit with a sheer navy-blue sarong and a pair of white wedge sandals, and overall she felt pretty good. She was never going to be a stick figure, and she wasn't about to wear a bikini like she knew Ashley would, but Lottie only cared about the opinion of one person, and he'd seen her in a bathing suit lots of times.

After the party she was going to go home with Becca and spend the night, so she packed her overnight things, and at three o'clock she told her mom she was ready to leave. "You look so pretty," her mom told her as they headed to the car. "I just can't believe that my baby girl is headed off to the senior send-off and then to college in a few weeks."

Lottie had never known her mom to be nostalgic, so she wasn't sure how to answer. Not wanting to have an emotional breakdown, she simply said, "Thanks, Mom." To be honest, she was having a hard time believing it as well, but she was so excited for the prospect of her talk with Nick that everything else was taking a backseat. She'd make it a point to spend some quality time with her mom tomorrow, so they could talk about what the future held for both of them, but tonight was all about Nick.

Chapter 27

Now

Charlotte looked up at Becca as she accepted a glass of tea and said, "I'm having dinner with Nick on Tuesday."

Becca rubbed her hands together like a little girl and almost squealed. "There is a chance for the two of you then?" she asked. "I knew if you just—"

"Slow down, Becca. It's just dinner, and it's just so we can talk. I know that Nick feels badly about how things ended with us. He just wants the chance to apologize, and I'm finally ready to accept it. After that he'll go back to his life, but it's my life I need help with."

"Charlotte Louise Luce, look me in the eye and tell me you don't still have feelings for Nick. If you can assure me of that, we can discuss what kind of help you think your life needs."

For a moment everything was quiet, and softly Charlotte replied, "I don't know what my feelings for Nick are, Bec, but I know that I want a relationship like you have with Jared, and until I can let go of the past, I can't really move forward into the future. I want respect and commitment, tenderness and passion, and I mean toe-curling, heart-pounding passion, the kind that makes your body ache for more. I want to know that I'm loved if I'm a size eight or a size eighteen, and if I put on a black teddy, I want to see lust in my man's eyes, and I'm no longer willing to settle for anything less. Is that too much to ask for?"

"Definitely not, sweetie." Becca smiled. "Definitely not."

The remainder of the weekend was a success with Charlotte and Becca treating the kids to Chuck E. Cheese's for dinner on Saturday night and then sharing a big, healthy breakfast, with the promised coffee, on Sunday morning. Charlotte was just packing up her things to leave when Jared walked in. She watched in admiration as the hunky, golden-haired doctor held his wife and three kids in his arms and showered them with kisses and hugs. *This is what matters,* thought Charlotte, *and this is what I'm going to have.*

With promises to stay in touch, Charlotte kissed all five of the Tylers good-bye. Before leaving, she whispered in Jared's ear, "You're one in a million, Dr. Tyler, and I love how happy you make my friend."

Jared gave her a soft kiss on her forehead and whispered back, "We make each other happy, Charlotte, and trust me—the right guy for you is out there. You just have to be willing to believe it."

Chapter 28

Then

Lottie gave her mom a hug and reluctantly left the security of the car. She had waited all day for this, and now she was scared to death. Nick was going to be late because he had a swim team meeting in Jacksonville that morning, but he'd promised her he would be there by four. Looking around for Becca or Noah, she spotted them both at the volleyball courts and waved as she made her way over to them.

"Wow, Shortcake, you're looking mighty fine this afternoon," Noah said with a smirk.

Lottie knew Noah's comment was all in good fun, but she wasn't quite as prepared when Craig Jeffers, their class president, joined in with his thoughts. "Noah's right, Lottie," he said. "You look hot!"

Right at that moment, Ashley walked by and mumbled "Oh please" under her breath, which just added to Lottie's embarrassment and the blush creeping up her cheeks. Not wanting anyone to know how much Ashley's hurtful words could still bother her, she grabbed the volleyball instead and asked, "Who's up for a game?"

By the time Nick arrived, the party was in full swing, and people were still playing volleyball, swimming, or just hanging out with their friends. Everyone knew that this would be their last big get-together as a class, but they all pretended it was just another Anna Maria High School event.

Around six o'clock the steak bake started, and as class valedictorian Lottie got to go through the line first. She was really way too nervous to eat, but Becca and Noah were both on the serving end and piled her plate with way too much food. Of course, just as Lottie was looking for a place to sit, Ashley walked up behind her and, seeing her huge plate of food, made noises like a snorting pig behind her back. Lottie didn't know if anyone else heard or not, but whatever appetite she had disappeared at that moment. When Nick sat down beside her, she smiled at him and tried to turn back the river of acid rolling in her stomach, but between her anxiousness over their upcoming conversation and Ashley's continuing snide remarks, she felt like she was fighting a losing battle.

As soon as dinner was over, Nick took her hand and said he was going to go play cards with some of the guys but would meet her at the pool house at eight. The look he gave her replaced the acid in her stomach with butterflies, and she knew without a doubt that the butterfly feeling was one she could get used to.

Time seemed to drag by, and with both Becca and Noah cleaning up from dinner, Lottie felt edgy and alone. It wasn't like she didn't have other friends in the class, because she did, but Nick, Noah, and Becca were her best friends and the ones she needed when she was tense. But Nick couldn't help, because he was the root of the tension, and Becca and Noah were on KP, so she walked around the beach-club grounds until seven fifty p.m. and then headed over to the pool house.

Lottie's hands were visibly shaking—heck, her whole body was shaking—so she grabbed a can of Coke from the cooler to have something to hold on to. Cautiously she stepped into the pool house. When she heard voices, she realized for the first time that maybe what Nick wanted to tell her wasn't something good. She recognized one of the voices as Nick's, so she moved on into the room, and for a moment the whole world just stopped.

There on the sofa was Nick, her Nick, with his swim trunks down around his ankles and Ashley kneeling beside him, her bikini top lying on the floor, ready to take him into her mouth. Lottie had only seen naked men in pictures, so she was not prepared for the shock of the magnificence or the magnitude of the boy she loved. Without thinking she gasped and automatically covered her mouth with her hands, dropping her Coke on the floor. The unopened can exploded, causing Nick to jump up and see Lottie just as Ashley turned around.

"Get lost, Lottie Loser," Ashley spat out with a malicious grin, and Lottie took off, running faster than she ever thought possible. Her heart was breaking, and everything she believed in was crashing down around her. In those few seconds she made a decision that would alter the course of her future for many years to come.

Chapter 29

Now

As Charlotte dressed for work on Monday, she thought back over the previous week and everything that had happened. It had been a whirlwind, that was for sure, but she was determined that this week would be better. Her personal life was usually so mundane that she was truly embarrassed by some of the things that had played out, but everyone was allowed a blip every decade or so, right?

So, putting on a very tailored and professional cream-colored Max Mara jacket dress and chocolate-brown pumps, she once again felt and looked like a market president of Olde Florida Bank. Rich brown pearls adorned her ears and wrist, and as always, her silver locket from Gran was around her neck. "I doubt if you would have been very proud of me last week, Gran," Charlotte said as she fastened the necklace. "But I know you would have supported me, and that's what got me through. I miss you so much." And then kissing her fingertips and touching them to her locket, she was out the door.

"Hey, boss lady," Carol said as Charlotte walked in the bank. "How was the weekend after your food poisoning episode?"

Friday seemed like a lifetime ago, and Charlotte had totally forgotten leaving early under the ruse of food poisoning. Her face immediately turned beet red, and she headed to her office mumbling *"Shit, shit, shit"* under her breath. After a moment at her desk, breathing deeply to get her composure back, Charlotte called Carol into her office. She didn't want to be dishonest with Carol, so she had to come clean. She gave Carol a soft smile and motioned for her to sit down. "I didn't have food poisoning, Carol," she stuttered. "I was hungover." *There, that wasn't so hard, was it?* she thought.

"Uh, I kind of knew that," Carol said, squirming in her seat. "My brother, Tony, was at the Crab Shack on Thursday night too, and he called me when he saw Noah and his hot brother helping you out. I was really just pulling your chain when you came in. Please don't be mad at me."

"I'm not mad at you, Carol, but I am disappointed in my behavior. The fact that any of our clients could have seen me like that, well, it's inexcusable." Charlotte put her head in her hands and thought, *So much for a better week.*

But Carol wasn't about to let her give in to those kinds of feelings. "Charlotte," she said softly, "we've all done things that we're not proud of, things we wish we could undo, but you are a great banker, a great boss, and you've been a champion for this community. Don't let one night of letting your hair down take that away from you."

Charlotte was speechless and a little embarrassed. "Thank you, Carol. That means a lot to me, but I still hope that no one else witnessed my lack of judgment on Thursday." She was just about to stand up and signal the end of the meeting when Carol spoke up again.

"Can I ask a question about Peter?" she posed tentatively.

Charlotte's eye started to twitch, but she said, "Okay, I guess. What about Peter?"

"Well, about four o'clock on Friday he called asking for you, and in all the time you've been going out, he's never called the main bank line. When I told him you had gone home sick, he sounded let down but then asked if you had gotten the roses he had sent. Anyway, given the fact that you were out drinking with the gorgeous Greysons on Thursday, instead of your standing date with Peter, and judging by your reaction when the flowers arrived, I kind of put two and two together and figured that you guys had a fight. Is everything okay?" Carol dropped her head, afraid to look Charlotte in the eye.

Charlotte let out a big sigh but once again decided to be honest. "We did have a disagreement. A big disagreement. I appreciate you telling me that he called, but now I think we both need to get to work." This time she did stand, and Carol understood the conversation was over.

At three o'clock every other Monday all the market presidents of Olde Florida Bank had a phone conference to discuss their loan pipelines, as well as any closed loans for the period. Charlotte was excited to share not only her shopping center opportunity but two other commercial loans she had closed and the fact that the Greyson marina loan was finally out of the red and back on track. She received lots of kudos from both the CEO, Martin Riggs, and the chief credit officer, Eric Short, so when six o'clock rolled around, she was in a great mood and feeling once again like she was in control of her destiny. Grabbing her bag and her keys, she said good night to the custodian and headed home with plans to do laundry.

After a quick stop at the organic market to pick up a roasted chicken and a salad, Charlotte was just walking in the door when the phone rang. She was in such a good mood that she didn't even think about what time it was or even what day it was until she looked at the phone and saw Peter's face and number on the screen. The last thing she wanted was to ruin her euphoria by talking to Peter, but she was an adult, and she could handle this.

"Charlotte Luce," she said formally into her cell phone. Ouch! Even she could feel the chill of that reception.

"Hi, Charlotte," Peter said, as if it were a normal Monday at six thirty. "How was your weekend with Becca?"

"Um, it was lovely, Peter. How was your cycling event?" *Really?* she thought. *We're going to make small talk after what happened on Thursday?*

"It was good, lots of exercise and beautiful scenery. I had a great time, but to be honest I would have enjoyed it more if we hadn't had our spat the other night. I met an old friend of yours from high school on the trip, Craig Jeffers, and he helped me understand the situation

77

with Nick better. I want you to know that I forgive the impulsive things that you said, and I'm willing to put them behind us."

If she didn't need her phone for work, Charlotte would have thrown it across the room. "You forgive me, Peter?" she spat out. "And just what did good old Craig tell you that makes you willing to bestow me with this charitable offering?"

"Now, Charlotte, you need to calm down. You aren't listening to me, but if you will, you'll know that this is a good thing. You told me before that Nick broke your heart, but you never told me what happened. Craig told me the whole story, so now I understand a lot of things better and can help you with some of your issues, which will help our relationship. Now isn't that what we both want?"

Charlotte wasn't sure what the penalty for murder was in the state of Florida, but if Peter had been anywhere near her, she was pretty certain she would have found out. She was angry and embarrassed, but mostly she felt foolish for wasting the last year of her life on a self-centered ass like Peter. "Charlotte?" he asked hopefully. "Can you hear me?"

As calmly as possible under the circumstances she took a deep breath and then said, "Yes, Peter, I can hear you, and now you need to hear me. I'm not sure that I've ever been as disappointed or disillusioned with anyone as I am with you right now. I am the judge and jury in this case, Counselor, and your summation and closing arguments just lost you the case."

"But, Charlotte," Peter started to plead.

"Overruled," she said with authority. "And it will be in your best interest if you just keep your mouth shut. Now, I'm going to end this call and delete your information from my contacts, and I suggest you do the same with mine. And in case there is any confusion, let me make it perfectly clear. We. Are. Done." And with that she ended the call.

"So much for my great day," she said with a sigh. Laundry still needed done, though, and hopefully a run would help her calm down, so she threw some things into the washer and changed into shorts and a T-shirt and took off. Forty-five minutes later she was tired and sweaty but relaxed and ready to think about spending her first evening with Nick in twelve years.

Chapter 30

Then

After running away from the beach club as if her life depended on it, Lottie realized that her cell phone was in her bag and she had no way to even call Becca to come get her. Weaving between houses and climbing a fence or two, just in case anyone had tried to follow her, she finally arrived home only to remember that her mom was gone for the night. Luckily, she knew there was a spare key hidden under a rock in the garden, and it was just light enough out to find it. She let herself into the dark house and stumbled around until she found the phone on the wall in the kitchen. She dialed Becca's cell, and when her friend answered, the resolve she had been clutching to started to crumble.

"Oh my gosh, Lottie, where are you?" Becca cried. "Nick took off after you like a madman, Ashley's telling some kind of wild story, and Noah looks like he wants to throttle her … What happened?"

Lottie had never felt so humiliated in her life. Wasn't it bad enough that she'd had to witness Nick and Ashley together? For the whole class to know was more than she could bear.

"Becca, I need your help, so quit crying and listen to me, please. I'm at my house, but no one can know that. Stay and clean up from the party just as you planned to do and tell anyone who asks about me that I'm at your house talking with your mom. That ought to be enough to keep anyone from trying to contact me. Do you understand?"

Becca was having a hard time calming down, but she took a deep breath and said, "I understand what you're saying; I just don't understand why. Can't you tell me what's going on?"

"Becca, please, you are the only person I can count on. My bag with my cell is still there, and I need it. After cleanup is done, act like you're going home but come here. Call me when you're about a block away. We need to meet, and I'll tell you more then, okay? Promise me, Bec, that you'll do this for me."

"Okay, Lottie. You know that I'll do whatever you want. The party is kind of fizzling out anyway, so I should be done here in about an hour."

"Thank you, Becca. I don't know what I would do without you." Lottie hung up the phone.

Before she allowed the tears in her eyes to fall, she made one more phone call. "Hi, Gran, it's me, Lottie, and well… Oh, Gran, I need you."

Chapter 31

Now

Tuesday was another gorgeous morning on the west coast of Florida, and Charlotte woke up feeling lighter and more relaxed than she had in months. Standing up for herself, at least in her personal life, had never been her strong suit. Even though she felt a tiny bit of remorse for being so hard on Peter, she was proud of herself and ready to start a new chapter in her life.

After a great meeting with the developers of the new shopping center, Charlotte set the principal owners up with Carol to start the new-account process. Then she worked on some credit reports before taking a late lunch to run over to Irene's to look for something new to wear to dinner with Nick. She knew she didn't really need something new, but she justified her clothes obsession with the fact that growing up she hadn't had the figure or the means for designer fashion. Her mom had bought their clothes at consignment stores, and Charlotte had vowed that when she grew up, she would never wear secondhand again.

After trying on several outfits, she decided on a lime-green sundress with a matching white-and-green-print shrug. Even though it was in the heat of summer, restaurants usually had the air so low a sweater or jacket was necessary, so it didn't take much to convince herself that it was a necessary expense. Besides, she had a new pair of mini-spike mesh Louboutin high-heeled sandals that would go perfectly with it, and Nick was one of the few people she could wear heels with and not feel like an Amazon.

Around three o'clock, just as she was finishing up some reports for the board of directors, Carol called into her office. "It's one of the gorgeous Greysons on line one, boss," she chuckled.

Charlotte could feel her blush all the way down to her toes. "Thank you, Carol," she replied, trying to put a little reprimand in her voice, but she was pretty sure Carol wasn't picking up on it. She took a deep breath to compose herself and put her phone on speaker. "Charlotte Luce."

"Hey, Madame President," came a deep voice from the other end. "We're still on for tonight, right?"

"May I ask whom I'm speaking with?" Charlotte teased.

"Ouch!" Nick responded, but Charlotte could feel his smile. "And here I thought the sight of me in my workout gear would have made a lasting impression on you."

"Oh, it's you, Nick. I hate to burst your bubble, but I see men in less almost every day. After all, this is Florida."

"Very funny, Charlotte. I don't remember you being so quick to banter, but I have to admit I kind of like it. I'm hoping this means that you aren't backing out on our date tonight."

Date? Was that different than just having dinner and sorting out their past? Now she was nervous and tongue-tied and didn't know what to do. She was so lost in her own thoughts that she almost missed hearing Nick say, "I'll pick you up at seven so we can watch the sun go down over the bridge, okay?"

"Okay, seven o'clock, I'll see you then." Without waiting for him to reply, she hung up the call.

Chapter 32

Then

By the time Becca arrived with her bag, Lottie had made her plans and talked with her mom. The hard part now was trying to make her friend understand.

"What do you mean you're going to leave for Indiana in the morning? You still have two weeks before you planned to leave for Gran's and three before you have to be at IU. You can't just up and leave like this. Please, Lottie. What did Nick say to you that's making you want to run away?"

The last thing that Lottie wanted to do was hurt Becca, but she knew that she couldn't stay. "Becca, it isn't what Nick said but what I saw. I don't want to relive it, but evidently, he and Ashley are together now, and he just didn't have the guts to tell me. I've always known how cruel Ashley is, but I never thought Nick would humiliate me like this. Anyway, you just have to trust me. I have to go, but I'm so sorry that I can't be here to finish out the summer with you."

Becca looked shell-shocked. "Lottie, that can't be right. Nick wouldn't be with Ashley, not after the way she's treated you. Maybe you misunderstood."

"Becca, they were half-naked. I didn't misunderstand anything," Lottie cried, no longer able to hold back her tears. "I'm a coward, I admit it, but right now, I don't ever want to see Nick or Ashley again."

Wiping her eyes and trying to regain her composure, she continued, "My mom is coming home and taking me to the airport early in the morning, but no one is to know that. You need to go to your house, but I'm going to sleep here tonight so I can get some things packed up."

Becca started crying in earnest, and the two girls hugged as if they would never see each other again. "Our lives are never going to be the same, Lottie; you know that, don't you?"

"They may never be the same, but our friendship always will be," Lottie said, wiping her nose. "You're the sister I never had Becca, and I love you just as if you were. Now, please, go home, and I'll call you as soon as I get to Gran's. I promise."

Chapter 33

Now

Charlotte prided herself on being the last one to leave the bank every evening, but today she had her desk locked and was ready to leave shortly after five thirty. Whether her dinner with Nick was a date or just a talk to clear the air, she was determined to look good and needed some extra time to primp.

There wasn't time to wash and dry her long, wavy locks, so she wrapped her hair in a turban and turned the shower on to get nice and steamy. More than anything she wanted a big glass of wine, but with her resolve to cut back on alcohol and the need to stay clearheaded tonight, she opted for a glass of mineral water with lime instead.

Grabbing her Josie Maran vanilla-pear, sugar scrub, she stepped under the extra-large tropical-rain shower-head and exfoliated and cleansed her skin until it was smooth and soft. While her skin was still warm, Charlotte followed her routine with another Josie favorite, her vanilla-pear, illuminating body butter. When finished, her skin was glowing with just a hint of bronze.

Remembering Nick's comment about a walk on the beach, Charlotte ran a straightener over her waves and pulled her hair into a high ponytail to help ward off frizz. With a touch of bronzer over her cheeks, soft peach gloss on her lips, and a double coat of lash-thickening mascara, she was ready to step into the new dress and sandals.

"Well, what do you think, Gran?" Charlotte asked, inspecting herself in the mirror as she fastened her locket around her neck. "When I stepped off the plane that afternoon twelve years ago, did you ever think Nick and I would be able to sit down together and talk?" Charlotte wasn't really expecting an answer, but her conversations with Gran had helped her over the years. Even if they might seem a little strange, they gave her the confidence and security that only her grandmother had ever been able to provide.

Chapter 34

Then

Lottie had been at IU for two weeks before the reality of life set in. The schoolwork came easily, but once she had arranged her dorm room the way she wanted it and acclimated herself to campus, she realized how alone she was. No mom to come home to at night, no giggling with Becca over hot fudge sundaes at Two Scoops, and, most of all, no Nick. Her heart felt as if it had curled up into a ball that was bouncing around trying to escape her chest, and she had no idea what to do to make it stop.

On the way to the airport that August morning, Lottie broke down and told her mom what she had seen. She'd figured if anyone could handle hearing about a sexcapade, it was Maggie Luce, but Lottie misjudged the protective instinct a mother, even her mother, has for her child. Lottie wasn't sure what she had expected, but it was not the anger she'd seen in her mom's eyes.

"Why, that son of a bitch!" her mom had exploded. "I have half a mind to go have a talk with him… and his dad."

Lottie groaned. "No, Mom, please. Promise me you'll leave this alone. I only told you so you would understand why I have to leave, not so you would do anything. I'm already humiliated. Promise me you won't say anything."

The agony on her daughter's face broke Maggie's heart. She knew how badly it hurt to lose love, and although her lost love had been for a much different reason, she wasn't about to do anything to hurt Lottie more. She gave Lottie a slow smile and squeezed her hand. "I promise, Lottie; your secret is safe with me. But always know you can talk to me about this if you need to, okay?"

Lottie nodded, but this was a conversation she didn't want to have with her mom again. Instead she took the truth of what had happened between Ashley and Nick and cleaned it up to a PG rating so she could talk with Gran. There was no way she could even say the words to describe to Gran what she had really witnessed, but she did need her guidance. In the new story, all clothing was left on, and the oral contact had been with mouths. Unfortunately, Lottie knew in her heart that might have only made it worse.

Chapter 35

Now

Charlotte grabbed her shrug and purse, and just as she stopped for one more look in the mirror, she heard a knock on the door. All of a sudden a panic attack started to well up, and she was overcome with emotion. *What am I doing?* she questioned herself, trying to get some air back in her lungs. *Can I sit down with Nick after all these years and just leave the hurt behind?* She reached up and grabbed her locket as the knocking on the door got louder. Out of nowhere a calm came over her, and she knew she was doing the right thing.

"Wow!" Nick exclaimed as she opened the door. "You look lovely and nothing like any banker I've ever had."

Charlotte smiled sweetly, and for the first time she was really looking forward to spending time with him.

He guided her to the passenger door of his Jeep and pointed out the open roof. "It's such a nice evening that I left the top down, but I can have it on in a minute if it's a problem."

Silently applauding herself for the decision to put her hair up, Charlotte just replied, "It's perfect."

Everything on Anna Maria Island was fairly close, so Charlotte knew it wouldn't take them long to get to the City Pier. She looked over at the handsome man sitting next to her and realized for the first time that she really didn't know anything about him. Did he have a girlfriend? Why had he joined the FBI? When was he going to leave and go back to his real life in Tampa?

Almost as if he could read her mind, Nick looked over at her and smiled. "It looks like some pretty serious thinking going on behind that beautiful face of yours. What's going on?"

All her thoughts seemed a little too personal, so she told a little white lie instead. "Just wondering about your dad and if you've found out what's going on with his finances yet." It seemed like an innocent question, especially since her bank was involved, but she swore she could see Nick's jaw tense.

"We have some ideas," he said with a big sigh, "but let's not talk business tonight, okay?"

Charlotte nodded but added, "If you need anything from the bank, you'll let me know, right? I want to help if I can."

At that moment Nick pulled into a parking space on the beach, and all talk of the issues at the marina was ended. He opened her door and took her hand, giving her a smile that melted her all the way down to her toes. "I've really been looking forward to this," he said. He kept her hand firmly clasped in his as they walked up the pier.

The restaurant wasn't too busy on Tuesday nights, so the hostess was able to seat them right away. It had been a long time since Charlotte had been to the City Pier, and as she looked out at the amazing view of the Sunshine Skyway Bridge, she couldn't remember why she had stayed away. Maybe it was because the menu didn't offer as many light offerings as she preferred, or maybe it was because Peter found it a little too plebeian, but deep down she knew it was because she couldn't come here without thinking of Nick. It had been one of their favorite places to eat when they were in high school, and having to push both french fries and Nick out of her mind at one time was just too hard.

When the waitress came by for their drink order, Charlotte decided she needed to keep all her wits about her, so she ordered a Diet Coke with lime, even though a tall glass of chardonnay sounded better. She was surprised when Nick ordered the same. As if he could read her mind, he said, "Alcohol has caused me to make some poor decisions in the past, and I don't want to make any mistakes tonight."

What's that all about? Charlotte thought, but remembering her own alcohol-induced performance just a few days before, she simply nodded in agreement.

"So, tell me about your visit with Becca," Nick said. "Did you have a good time?"

Charlotte's face lit up when she started to talk about Becca and her family. "It was just what I needed," Charlotte sighed. "Becca and Jared are the most down-to-earth and loving couple I've ever known, and their kids are adorable. I never leave there without feeling good inside."

"I still can't believe Becca is married," Nick said, shaking his head. "I thought she was all set to attend Ave Maria and go into nursing so she could become a nun and be a part of the Mother Teresa Project. How did she end up married and with kids no less?"

"I guess all it took was the right man," Charlotte answered honestly. "The moment she met Jared, I knew that the convent was going to be short one fine nun."

"And how about you, Charlotte?" Nick asked in a deeper voice than usual. "You never found the right man to settle down with?"

Looking down at her drink instead of at Nick, she replied honestly, "Evidently it's a trait I inherited from my mom." Thankfully the waitress came then to take their orders, because the last thing Charlotte wanted to discuss with Nick Greyson was her love life, or, to be honest, her lack of one. He had already witnessed the debacle with Peter, and that was more than enough for him to know.

While they waited on their shrimp baskets and mango coleslaw, Charlotte decided it was time to put Nick on the hot seat. "So, supermodel Stella Harper, huh?"

Charlotte couldn't ever remember seeing Nick blush, but for just an instant, the tiniest bit of red crept up his face. He recovered quickly and said cockily, "You have been keeping tabs on me."

Now it was Charlotte's turn to blush, and she couldn't turn it off as easily. "What? No, definitely not, but I do buy groceries, and your picture was on the cover of every gossip magazine last spring. 'Local Hero Engaged to Senator's Supermodel Daughter' was pretty much the lead copy on all of them."

92

Nick laughed, actually laughed, and Charlotte could feel the heat rising in her face. Pushing her food to the middle of the table, she was just about to tell him she wanted to leave when he reached across the table and took her hand. "Stella's a nice kid, Charlotte, but we were never engaged. It was all a publicity stunt cooked up by her manager after I caught the man who was stalking her, but I promise you neither one of us had any feelings other than friendship for the other."

He held her hand firmly in his and looked up at her with his gorgeous blue eyes, and the heat that had been on her face was now traveling through her body. *Shit, shit, shit!* she thought. *Get a grip!*

"Truce?" he asked, but deep down he was pleased that Charlotte had been bothered by the thought of him engaged to another woman. But then it hit him that maybe she didn't care that he might have been engaged and just didn't like that he had laughed at her. One way or another, he knew he was going to have to tread lightly if he was going to get the night back on track. He had messed up big time with her before, and he had no intention of doing it again.

Chapter 36

Then

Life at IU had finally settled in, and Lottie was making the best of it. She missed Becca a lot, but her suite mates, Ellen and Cristi, were great, and the three of them got along together really well. Both girls were from Indiana and couldn't understand why Lottie would choose to leave the warmth of Florida for the certainty of the snow and ice in their home state, but they came to understand how important it was for her to be nearer to her gran.

Just before Halloween Ellen came rushing in their dorm room one Friday afternoon full of excitement. "Theta Xi is having a big Halloween party tonight to welcome all freshmen. Isn't that awesome? I've so been wanting to go to a real fraternity party, and now we can!"

Cristi and Ellen were talking about what they were going to wear and how to fix their hair when Lottie spoke up. "It's time I went by Charlotte," she told her friends. "Lottie is the little girl who lived in a dream world, but Charlotte is the woman who wants to see what the world is all about, and I start the journey tonight!"

The party was in full swing when the girls arrived, and they were all overwhelmed by how many people were there and how freely the beer was flowing. After her declaration of independence, Lottie accepted a beer from the first guy who offered her one and moved with him out onto the dance floor. She hated the strong bitter taste of the drink, but before she knew it, her first cup was empty, and another had been put in her hand. She wasn't sure she was even dancing with the same guy, but what did it matter as long as she was experiencing life, right? To be honest, the room was looking a little fuzzy. She downed her beer, thinking maybe she was just hot, and when another one was given to her, she took it without hesitation.

All of a sudden, the room started to swim, but before she could fall down, strong, masculine arms grabbed ahold of her. "Hey, baby, are you okay?" came a voice from above. Lottie looked up into the eyes of a very good-looking guy, and when he offered to take her someplace where she could be more comfortable, she didn't hesitate. He helped her up the stairs to the back of the fraternity house and led her into his bedroom.

"What's your name, baby?" the guy asked Lottie as he moved his hands under her shirt and very close to her bra.

"It's Charlotte," she answered, "Charlotte Luce."

"I'm Kyle," the guy replied as he unzipped his pants. "Have you ever given a senior a blow job?"

Lottie had never even really kissed a boy, let alone do *THAT* to them, but hey, wasn't it time she found out what all the fuss was about? She didn't want to die a virgin, and she had to start somewhere.

Kyle pushed Lottie onto her knees and pulled his, well, you know out of his pants. She was a little disappointed. It was standing up, that's for sure, but it wasn't nearly as big and beautiful as Nick's had been. She was just kneeling there comparing the two when Kyle grabbed her hair and forced her open mouth onto him. *Now what?* she thought, but Kyle, always the gentleman, helped her out.

"Suck it," he ordered, and she did. Kyle was moaning and holding her by the hair, but Lottie's jaw was getting very tired, and the three beers she had consumed were really fighting in her stomach. She tried to let Kyle know that she needed to stop, but he just kept holding on and moaning, and then all of a sudden…, she threw up.

"What the fuck?" Kyle yelled. "You fucking bitch, get the hell out of our house!" Lottie looked down, and his pants, shoes, and once-erect member, which now hung limply, were all covered in her vomit. She was mortified. Kyle continued to rant, and his friends came in to see what was going on. She hung her head and ran down the stairs and all the way back to the dorm. It wasn't until she was safely back in her room that she realized it had happened again. Would she ever be able to see a man's thing naked without having to run away?

The hardest part was facing people on campus after that. She might have left the nickname Lottie Loser back home on Anna Maria Island, but by the next morning the name Charlotte Puker had circulated around the Greek community, and her chances of reinventing herself were pretty much nonexistent.

Chapter 37

Now

Deciding that a change of topic was in order, Nick asked Charlotte about her job. "What made you decide to go into banking?" he asked with sincerity. "You always talked about accounting, so I thought you would have gone that direction."

"As a matter of fact, my degree is in accounting," Charlotte said, "and I actually was working for a large accounting firm in Indianapolis when I got my MBA. But once Gran died, Indiana just didn't feel like where I was supposed to be."

"I was sorry to hear about your grandmother, Charlotte," Nick said softly. "Noah called me as soon as he heard, and I wish now I would have done something, but I didn't think you would want to hear from me."

He looked up at her with such hope in his eyes that she couldn't tell him it would have only made the hurt worse if he had contacted her, so she just nodded and tried to hold back her tears. "Thanks, Nick, I appreciate that. Gran was an amazing lady, and she left me with wonderful memories and my little bungalow on the beach. Even though she loved having me close by, she always knew I'd come home to Anna Maria someday. What about you? You always wanted to be the kick-ass, cool teacher who helped kids love history and competitive swimming. Where did the FBI come into that dream?"

Nick looked down at her trusting face and knew he couldn't tell her the truth. Teaching had been his dream when they were young and thought they would both come back to the island after college, but after what had happened at the senior send-off and her running away without giving him a chance to explain, he had changed his major and decided criminal justice was the way to go. One of his professors had suggested he apply to the FBI training facility at Quantico after he graduated, and from there everything had fallen in place.

"It just kind of happened," he answered. "I guess I was in the right place at the right time" Holding out his hand, he asked, "Now are those shoes sand worthy, because you promised me a walk on the beach?"

While Nick paid the check, Charlotte walked out to the pier and slipped off her shoes. Smiling up at him as he joined her, she showed him the fancy sandals in her hand and said, "I may not own a pair of shoes that I would wear to walk in the sand, but I have two perfectly good feet."

"When did you become such a diva?" he laughed.

"It's just another part of being all grown up," she sassed and then took off running down the beach, Nick racing after her.

"Okay, okay, I surrender," Nick said, laughing and holding his side. "I forget that for a girl you're a pretty good runner, and you forget that I ate all my shrimp plus half of yours."

"For a girl?" Charlotte squealed. "I would have thought by now some woman would have taught you some manners."

"Nope," he replied, "but I'm a willing student." He winked at her, and for a few minutes they walked the beach as if twelve years hadn't passed since their last beach walk together, and everything felt right with the world.

Finally, Nick grabbed her hand and turned her around to face him. He didn't want to spoil the magic of the moment, but he knew they couldn't go forward until they got their talk out of the way. Rubbing his thumb over the soft skin of her fingers and looking into her big green eyes, he was pissed as hell that he had taken down some of the biggest criminals in the country without issue but that trying to talk with this fiery woman had his insides doing backflips off the high dive.

"Lottie," he started, "I mean Charlotte, we need to talk about what happened at the senior send-off. You know that, right?"

Kicking at the sand like a five-year-old, she replied, "I guess."

"You guess?" Now Nick was getting worked up. "For twelve years I've thought about how much I wanted, no, *needed* to explain to you about that night. I was hoping it was something you wanted too."

"What is there really to explain, Nick?" she asked. "You said you had something to talk with me about that night, and either you and Ashley decided to tell me as a team, or I walked in sooner than you planned, but believe me, I understood. You wanted me to know that you and Ashley were together. Well, I got the picture, loud and clear!" Now Charlotte was getting upset, but when she tried to pull her hand away, he wouldn't let go.

Nick looked at her as if she were an alien. "Please tell me that you did not just say that you believed that I was going to tell you that Ashley and I were a couple. After all the crap she put you through, you honestly thought so little of me that—"

Not allowing him to finish his sentence, Charlotte jumped in. "But she was hot, Nick, and she'd wanted you since we were in the fifth grade. Girls like that don't give up, and she obviously had hidden talents. It hurt when I was seventeen, but I'm an adult now, and I understand." *Like hell I understand!* she thought.

Charlotte continued trying to pull away, but Nick held on tighter and shook his head. "How could you not have known that I was in love with you?"

"What? That isn't even funny, Nick. You told me you had some big thing you wanted to share with me, and instead I walked in on Ashley about to…" She knew her face was scarlet because the minute the words "big thing" were out of her mouth, she remembered Nick's big thing and Ashley licking her silicone-injected lips.

"Charlotte, didn't you ever wonder why I never went on dates and instead spent all my time with you?"

"Well, we were friends, and besides, I thought that when you and Noah had those mystery nights out you were seeing girls from other schools but didn't want to talk about them in front of me."

"There were no other girls, Charlotte, at least for me, although Noah did have his share. Those mystery nights were visits to our mom over at Siesta Key. She and husband number three had a condo there, and it was Pop's feelings we were protecting, not yours."

"None of this makes any sense, Nick," she said, shaking her head. "We were just friends, and besides, boys weren't really interested in me back then."

Charlotte was trembling so Nick reached down and clasped both of her hands in his. "We quit being just friends about the day after we met," he said with confidence, "and the reason you didn't think boys were interested in you was because they all knew you were mine."

Charlotte's heart was beating a million miles a minute, and she was afraid she was going to hyperventilate. She had been in love with Nick, and now he was telling her he had been in love with her too? If she had taken his calls and not run to Indiana so fast, would things have been different? This was too messed up, even for her, and she had absolutely no idea what to do. She reached up and touched her locket and silently asked Gran for help. *I'm in deep, Gran,* she pleaded. *Why didn't I listen to you?*

Chapter 38

Then

After the Halloween-party fiasco Lottie started spending her weekends at the farm with Gran. She'd ride the bus to Martinsville on Friday after class, and Gran would bring her back to campus on Sunday evenings. Lottie would have been content to do that her entire college career if Gran hadn't put a stop to it after Thanksgiving break.

"Okay, Lottie," Gran said that Sunday morning of Thanksgiving weekend, "it's time you and I had a talk. You didn't come all the way to IU to spend all your weekends with me, and even though I love having you, it's time you told me what's going on."

There was no way in hell Lottie could tell her gran what had happened at the frat party, but she did tell her how lonely she felt at school and how much she missed her friends from Anna Maria. She even went as far as to say that she had tried to reinvent herself but it hadn't worked out so well.

"Lottie," Gran said with a smile, "I know I seem like an old lady to you, but believe it or not, I was young once too, and I understand about boys and love. I don't know what happened between you and Nick, but I do know that you need to talk to him and you need to forgive him. Holding on to your anger is only hurting you, and you can't move on until you can forgive."

Lottie loved her gran so much and trusted her completely, but she couldn't forgive Nick, and she truly believed Gran would understand if she knew what he had really done. Shaking her head, she said, "I just can't."

Gran never mentioned Nick again after that, but she also told Lottie that she needed to stay at school on most weekends and learn to enjoy college life. "I love you as if you were my own daughter, Lottie," Gran said with tears in her eyes, "and I hope someday you'll understand that when you try to hide from problems, they still find you in the end. It's always better just to face them head-on so they don't have any power over you." Then she wrapped her arms around her beautiful granddaughter, and for a few minutes they both held on tight.

Chapter 39

Now

It took every bit of courage Charlotte could muster, but she looked up into Nick's eyes and asked the question that had haunted her for twelve years. "So what was it you wanted to talk to me about that night then, Nick?" she asked with a vulnerability in her voice that she hated but couldn't control.

Nick's eyes were so dark they were almost navy blue. She knew he was hurting, but she was too, and there was no going back now. When he let go of her hands, she instantly missed the warmth and the security they had provided, and without thinking she reached up and touched his cheek. "Nick," she said softly, "will you tell me now, please?"

Covering the hand that was stroking his cheek, he gave her a half smile. "I feel as if I've waited a lifetime to have this talk with you, and now I'm scared shitless," he said. "Maybe we've had enough revelations for one night?"

"No." Charlotte surprised herself with her strength, but she knew in her heart it was time to get everything out in the open. "I need to know now," she continued, "and putting it off won't change a thing. Please, Nick."

He knew he couldn't deny her, he never could, but somehow the longings he'd had as an eighteen-year-old seemed hard to put into words twelve years later. Taking her hand again, he said, "Let's walk down to the park and find a bench. I think I need to sit down for this."

The park at this end of the beach was virtually empty this time of night, so they easily found a glider and sat down. Charlotte was full of restless energy, and without thinking she started pushing her bare foot in the sand, propelling the swing back and forth. She knew that Nick needed to be the one to start the conversation. She tried to glance at him under her lashes to get a read on his face but was not at all prepared for the hammer that started pounding in her chest. Oh my gosh, Nick Greyson was one gorgeous man! The heat radiating off his long, lean body was starting to envelop her, and when he turned and touched her hand, she thought she would spontaneously combust. *Shit, shit, shit!* This was not good.

Nick cleared his throat and looked her in the eye, obviously uncertain how to begin. "I realize now that I made a lot of assumptions about us when we were younger. I mean, I knew how I felt, and I thought you felt the same way, but I was always too much of a chickenshit to come right out and say it. But the closer and closer it came for us to leave for college and be away from each other for months at a time, I knew I had to do something. That's why I asked you to meet me at the pool house the night of the send-off. I knew if I didn't do it then, it might be too late."

Charlotte was stunned, too stunned to even speak. She understood her insecurities, but Nick? He'd always seemed so confident and in control.

"Anyway," he continued, "I knew that your mom's, um, proclivities bothered you, and I didn't want to scare you off, but I wanted so badly to kiss you and to love you. I didn't have great role models in the relationship department either, so I just made myself be content with what we had. One day, Noah asked me what was going to happen when we left for school, and it hit me that I didn't want some other guy to share all those firsts with you. That's when I made my plan to tell you on the night of the send-off."

Charlotte willed the words out of her mouth. "And what exactly were you going to tell me?"

Nick ran his hands through his hair, looking for just the right words. "You know," he said huskily, "this all made perfect sense to me when I was eighteen, but now it seems a little crazy."

"Humor me," she replied.

"Well, I was going to ask you to wait for me, at least until Christmas break, before getting involved with someone else. I was hoping by then you would be sure I was the one, and we could be a real couple. I wanted to be your first everything, and instead I fucked it all up."

The pounding in her heart had returned, but now it was threatening to break her heart in two. How could something that should have been so special turn out so wrong?

"So where did Ashley come into the picture, Nick?" she asked softly. She didn't want to hurt him any deeper, but this was the last piece of the puzzle, and she needed it in place.

"I was really nervous when I got to the country club that day, so Noah gave me a beer first thing. I wasn't used to drinking, because I didn't want to get kicked off of the swim team, but I thought one would calm my nerves. Then when we were playing cards, the other guys were drinking, and before I knew it, I'd had six, which for a first-time drinker was a ton. Noah was aware of what was going on, so after the game he offered to help me take some candles and flowers to the pool house, and Ashley must have overheard us talking. I was just getting ready to light the candles when she came in. I swear, Charlotte, nothing happened. I didn't touch her, and she didn't touch me, but before I could even ask her what she was doing there, she had my swim trunks down and had pushed me down on the couch. If I hadn't had the beers, my reaction time would have been better, and for that I'll never forgive myself. When she heard you come in, she took off her top and got on her knees so it would look like…"

"She was giving you a blow job?" Charlotte said, remembering like it was yesterday the horrific hurt she'd felt at seeing Nick like that with Ashley.

Nick looked at her with surprise, as if he couldn't imagine those words coming out of her mouth. The surprise then turned to hurt, and

105

his eyes became stormy as he realized what Ashley's little trick had cost them both. "Yes," he said as he hung his head.

For a few minutes neither one of them said anything, and then Nick asked, "Is there a chance that Lottie can forgive me? Because I really want to get to know Charlotte."

Using her bare foot to get the glider swinging again, she took both of his hands in hers and looked up at the worry on his face. "I think she already has," she said with a smile, and together they watched the bright orange sun sink into the water.

Chapter 40

Then

Sophomore year, Ellen and Cristi moved into an apartment off campus. They'd asked Charlotte to join them, but her scholarship only allowed for her to live in the dorm, so she had to say good-bye to her two good friends. She knew she was always welcome to visit their apartment, and she would, but if felt like leaving Anna Maria all over again.

The one upside was she was asked to be a resident adviser, which meant a suite to herself, but she wondered how in the world she was going to be able to advise anyone else when her own life was such a joke. Plus, the incoming freshmen were for the most part the same age she was, and she told herself if she was lucky she might learn a thing or two.

Charlotte spent one weekend a month, as well as holidays, with Gran, but by the middle of the year she had met some new people. Even though she didn't have any actual dates, she was part of a group of girls and guys who hung out together, and she had finally started to enjoy life as a coed.

Just after Christmas break of Charlotte's senior year at IU, Ryan Noble breezed into her life and turned it upside down. She was interning at an accounting firm in Bloomington when Ryan walked into the office looking as if he had stepped off the cover of *GQ*. He said he had an appointment with her boss, and Charlotte asked him to have a seat until Mr. Saunders was available. Instead he introduced himself and looked her over as if she were the special on the dessert bar.

"I'm Ryan Noble," he said. "I don't believe we've met."

Charlotte could feel the color rushing to her cheeks, and she felt every bit of her young age. She couldn't tell whether he was flirting with her or just being friendly. He kept looking at her, so she answered. "I'm Charlotte Luce, Mr. Saunders's new intern," she mumbled. "I'm sure he won't be long if you'll please have a seat."

Charlotte was good with numbers, not with men. She really wished he would just sit down and quit looking at her, but wishes don't usually come true. Trying to be polite, she looked up and smiled, and crap, he was good-looking! With hair so black it shimmered and eyes that were a mix between gray and lavender, he was the most exotic-looking man Charlotte had ever seen.

About that time Mr. Saunders stepped out of his office, and Charlotte was able to breathe. "Ryan," he said, shaking the man's hand, "I apologize for the wait, but I had an urgent call from a client that took longer than I anticipated."

Giving Charlotte a wink, Ryan replied, "It was no problem at all. Charlotte here kept me company."

That only made Charlotte blush again and worry that her boss would think she had overstepped her bounds, but Mr. Saunders just smiled. "Yes, Charlotte was quite a catch," he said as he led Mr. Noble into his office.

Ryan turned around and, looking right at her, remarked, "Yes, I'm sure she would be," which scared Charlotte to death.

It was almost five thirty, and Charlotte was gathering up her things to leave for the day when a male voice behind her made her jump.

"I'm sorry," he laughed. "I thought you heard the door open." Charlotte looked up, and there was Ryan Noble in all his handsome glory with a sly smile on his face. "Have a drink with me, Charlotte," he said, more a command than a question.

"Um, I don't think Mr. Saunders would approve of that," she replied, hoping the use of her boss's name would do the trick, but Ryan was prepared for her refusal.

"I've already asked him, and he's fine with it, so unless you have a boyfriend who would object, I would love to buy you a drink and get to know you better." He flashed her a million-dollar smile, and Charlotte almost fainted. "Come on, Miss Luce, what do you say?" he asked.

With bees swarming all through her body, Charlotte just said, "Okay."

Drinks turned out to be coffee once Ryan realized that Charlotte wasn't twenty-one. Coffee turned into dinner, and before she knew it, the restaurant was closing, and Ryan was asking when he could see her again. It was the first time she had talked so much with a guy since Nick, and she was both excited and scared to death at the prospect of the date they set for the upcoming Friday night. The minute she got home, she called Ellen and Cristi to tell them the news but was not at all prepared for what they told her.

"Ryan Noble!" screamed Cristi. "You have a date with Indiana's most eligible bachelor, the chick magnet Ryan Noble?"

"What?" Charlotte answered. "You must have him mistaken with someone else. He's super good-looking and all, but he's really nice. I mean, it can't be who you're thinking of, can it?"

"Check your e-mail," chimed in Ellen. "I just forwarded you a picture from the *Indianapolis Star*. Is that the Ryan Noble you spent the evening with?"

Charlotte was in shock. Sure enough, her Ryan Noble had recently been named Indiana's most eligible bachelor by the *Indianapolis Star*, and in the picture he was arm in arm with a gorgeous blonde who made Charlotte feel like a country bumpkin. *Shit, shit, shit,* she thought. *Why does this keep happening to me?* The bubble of excitement over meeting Ryan and having such a nice evening was just about to burst with a big bang when she looked down at her e-mail and saw a message from him. *"I had a wonderful time tonight, and I look forward to Friday. Sweet dreams, Charlotte... Ryan."* And just like that, the bubble was back!

Three weeks later Ryan took Charlotte to a very exclusive restaurant for dinner and then invited her back to his house. She was pretty certain that this meant sex and had even talked with Ellen and Cristi ahead of time so she was prepared, but once he unlocked the front door, her nerves got the best of her, and she started to tremble.

"Hey, what's the matter?" Ryan asked as he wrapped her in his arms. "Are you cold?"

Charlotte put her head on his shoulder and blurted out, "I've never done this before."

"You've never been in a man's house before?" he asked.

Taking a deep breath and summoning all her strength, she pulled away and looked him in the eye. "I've never had sex before, but I want to—I mean if you want to, that is."

At almost thirty, Charlotte was sure that Ryan was used to women more worldly than she was, but at that moment, he was making her feel as if she was his everything and he was the luckiest man on earth. Taking her face in his hands, he kissed her, innocently at first but then with more passion and determination, the kisses becoming demanding and raw. He nipped at her bottom lip and then said, "Oh, I want to. I want to very much. But I need you to be sure. Your first time isn't something you get a do-over on."

Charlotte looked into his beautiful eyes and knew she had never wanted anything more. Once she was able to breathe again from the headiness of the kiss, she sighed, "I'm sure."

Chapter 41

Then

Ryan knew his way around a woman's body; Charlotte had to give him that. But she was pretty sure he wasn't used to playing tug-of-war with the sheets just to make contact with flesh. He had gotten her out of her clothes without a lot of effort, but moving forward was starting to be an uphill battle.

"Charlotte," he finally said, "I think this isn't really what you want at all, and we need to stop now before it gets any harder."

She looked at him with tears in her eyes and wondered if by "before it gets any harder" he was referring to the granite she could feel between his legs when he held her. "I'm so sorry," she cried. "I really do want this, but I'm scared, and I'm fatter than the girls you usually go out with, and my experience with guys hasn't been so great."

Ryan looked down at the innocence on her face, and his heart clenched. "You are gorgeous, Charlotte Luce, and there isn't a woman I know who can hold a candle to you. I want so much right now to make love to you, but instead we're going to lie here and hold each other, and you're going to relax. We've got all night."

The next morning Charlotte woke up relaxed, refreshed, and no longer a virgin.

Chapter 42

Now

When Wednesday morning rolled around, Charlotte felt as if the weight of the world had been lifted from her shoulders. She and Nick had talked, and she now understood what had really happened on that night twelve years ago, and they were friends again. Deep down, she knew it could never be the same kind of friendship they'd had when they were kids, but at least now she was ready to let go of the past and move on with her life.

She put on a yellow sheath dress and Christian Louboutin Debriditoe nude, patent leather pumps from her closet. She looked in the mirror and smiled at the reflection looking back. The dress looked like sunshine, matching Charlotte's sunny mood perfectly. With Gran's locket, a pair of silver hoop earrings, and a few Alex and Ani bracelets on her wrists, she was ready to head out for a great day of banking. But first, a rare treat from McDonald's—a vanilla iced coffee!

As usual Carol was already working when Charlotte arrived at seven thirty. Charlotte stopped at her desk and handed her an iced coffee of her own. "Thanks, boss lady," Carol said with a big smile. "What's the occasion?"

"I just wanted you to know how much I appreciate you," Charlotte replied, "and I'm in a really good mood!" With that she headed to her office and got busy on some much-needed paperwork to review.

A little after ten Carol called into her office. "I think your good mood is here to see you," she said teasingly. Charlotte looked up, and sure enough there was Nick in all his gorgeous glory. He was dressed very much like an islander in tan shorts and a white polo shirt, but oh, how his athletic body filled them out. After taking just a minute more to ogle him and to get her composure under control, she opened her door and went out to greet him.

"This is a surprise," she said. "Are you here to discuss your dad?"

Nick looked her up and down, and Charlotte couldn't help but blush. "No, I'm not here about Pop," he answered, "but I would like to talk if you have a minute."

Charlotte motioned toward her office and closed the door behind them. "Is everything all right?" she asked, wondering what could have happened since their epiphany the night before.

"Everything is great, but I just couldn't wait to see you again," Nick said, taking her hand. "I want to take you on a real date, Charlotte—that's why I'm here. If you're free on Friday, I thought we might drive up to Tarpon Springs and have dinner at Maya and Dimitri's restaurant. She's been begging me to come, and I think you would love it. What do you say?"

Charlotte was speechless. A real date? What did that mean? Evidently she was taking too long coming up with a reply, so Nick answered for her. "I'm going to take it as a 'Yes, Nick, I'd love to have dinner with you on Friday, and yes, I can leave a little early so we can be on the road by five thirty.'"

Charlotte shook her head and laughed. "Is being pushy another one of those things they taught you at G-man training?"

"Actually, I learned it from Noah, but I did learn all kinds of things at G-man training." The look he was giving Charlotte made her blush from head to toe, and that made Nick smile from ear to ear.

"It's a yes then?" he asked again. Charlotte nodded.

Chapter 43

Then

In two days Charlotte would be a college graduate! The four years at IU had gone by so quickly. Even though she was already enrolled at IU of Indianapolis to begin her MBA, she knew that this was a major milestone in her life. Her mom was even flying in from Arizona for the big day, so Charlotte needed to get up and showered so she could pick her mom up from the airport at two that afternoon.

Charlotte was ready to get on the road at eleven thirty. The drive to the Indianapolis airport would only take about an hour, but she wanted to get there early in case her mom's flight got in ahead of time. She started up her bright red Grand Prix, and as she always did when she drove, she remembered the day it had arrived. Her mom had made a huge jewelry sale and wanted to do something special for her only child, and a car had seemed just the thing. Charlotte loved the car, and it was special to her because it had come from her mom.

After finding a place to park, she entered the airport to wait for her mom's flight to arrive. She was about halfway through a Diet Coke and the newest *People* magazine when she heard a familiar voice behind her. "Excuse me," the voice asked, "do you know how I can get to Bloomington?"

Charlotte jumped up, almost spilling her drink, and screamed, "*Becca!* What are you doing here?"

"I couldn't let my best friend graduate from college without me, now could I?"

Tears ran down both girls' cheeks as they hugged and danced around. Then Charlotte felt a tap on her shoulder, and there stood her mom.

"Is this a private reunion, or is there room for one more?" she laughed.

"Oh, Mom," Charlotte cried as she held her mother close, "I can't believe you're here." Wiping a tear from her eye, she looked her mom and her best friend up and down and then laughed. "You two planned this, didn't you? This is the best graduation gift I could have asked for."

Becca and her mom just shrugged their shoulders and laughed, but it was obvious to anyone walking by that they were witnessing a moment of pure love.

Once they were settled in the car and back on the road, Maggie started in with questions about the upcoming weekend and when she was going to get to meet Ryan. Charlotte had told Becca that she and Ryan were sleeping together, but telling her mom felt different. She knew her mom would be okay with it, but it just seemed a little personal.

"Well," Charlotte said excitedly, "tonight is just for us, but tomorrow Ryan made reservations for us all to have dinner at his country club. Gran will be here in the afternoon, so you can all get to know him at once."

Maggie smiled, happy that her daughter had finally found someone special, but she did worry that the gap in their ages might become a problem. This was Charlotte's weekend, though, so she kept her thoughts to herself and sat back and listened to the two girls chat. Looking over at her beautiful and very grown-up daughter, she realized just how much she had missed being a part of Charlotte's life.

After a true girls' night on Thursday, Charlotte stayed at the hotel with her mom and Becca, and they all slept in on Friday morning. Maggie had coffee, juice, and pastries sent up to the room so they could enjoy a little more time together before Charlotte had commencement practice and Gran arrived. Soon it was time for Charlotte to go.

"Gran will be here around four," Charlotte said, grabbing her purse and her phone. "She knows her way around Bloomington, so she'll come here to you. I'll be back around five, and Ryan will be here at seven, so there should be plenty of time for us to all get ready." Looking again at her mom and her friend, Charlotte beamed. "I just can't tell you how much it means to have you both here." They had another group hug, and Charlotte was out the door, ready to feel for the first time what an IU graduation ceremony was like.

Ryan arrived right on time and looked good enough to eat. He was dressed in a dark-gray suit, with a dove-gray shirt and black striped tie, and Charlotte could tell the three women were impressed. Ryan was always charming without being arrogant, and by the time they were headed to the country club for dinner, they were all talking like old friends.

When the questions started to fly, Ryan reached over and squeezed Charlotte's hand, and she felt her heart skip a beat. The smile on his handsome face told her he was fine playing the game. Once again, she wondered what he was doing with her.

"So, Ryan, what do you do for a living?" her mom asked, even though Charlotte had already told her he was a stockbroker.

"Did you graduate from IU too?" chimed in Becca.

"Yes, I'm an IU alum."

"Does your family live close by?" was Gran's question, and yes, Ryan's parents had a home on Geist Reservoir in Indianapolis.

"It's a lovely place," Charlotte added with a smile, wanting Ryan to know how much it had meant to her when his mom had invited her to brunch a few weeks earlier.

Ryan had given Charlotte her graduation present a few days early because he wanted her to have it for her big day, and she lovingly touched the beautiful green stones of the bracelet while she listened in on the questions and answers.

"An emerald bracelet, Ryan?" she had gasped when she'd opened up the black velvet jeweler's box. "It's way too much."

Ryan had taken the bracelet and fastened it on her wrist. He rested his beautiful face against her forehead and said gently, "Emerald is the birthstone for May, and I never want you to forget the importance of this May and your college graduation. Besides, the green is the same color as your eyes, and I just couldn't resist."

Charlotte had thrown her arms around his neck, thanked him, and given him a long kiss of appreciation, which had led to an even-longer kiss, which had led to a night of thanksgiving for both of them.

They were about halfway through dinner the night before Charlotte's graduation when a ruggedly handsome blond man stopped at their table. "Ryan, how are you?" asked the hottie.

Ryan stood up and greeted his friend and introduced Charlotte, her family, and Becca. "This is Dr. Jared Tyler," he told the women. "We were fraternity brothers at IU."

Just the word *fraternity* had Charlotte remembering her freshman-year Halloween disaster, and her face began to heat. She looked around hoping no one had noticed, and sure enough they hadn't, because all eyes were on Becca and Dr. Tyler. In that one moment Charlotte knew that Becca's yearning to be a nun had just been replaced with a yearning of another kind, and she couldn't wait to get her friend alone so they could talk.

Saturday morning dawned sunny and clear, which for early May in Indiana was almost a miracle. The graduation took place at the IU football field, and after many hours of many names being called, Charlotte was holding her bachelor of science degree from the IU School of Business. She had graduated summa cum laude, and just shy of age twenty-one, she felt as if the world was her oyster.

After the ceremony, everyone took lots of pictures, and Gran pulled Charlotte aside and handed her a beautifully wrapped box. "I'm so proud of you, Lottie," Gran said, "and I know your dad would be proud of you too. I didn't get to see my boy graduate from college, but watching you today and being a part of your life has helped me to deal with a loss no mother should ever have to know."

Charlotte wiped the tears from her eyes and hugged the person who had most shaped her life. "I would have loved to have known my dad," she whispered. "I'm pretty certain he would have been a lot like you." She opened the box and pulled out a delicate silver chain holding a vintage silver locket. On the back of the locket was an inscription that Gran said was so Charlotte would always know her gran was with her in spirit, even if they weren't physically together.

"There's something else for you in the box," Gran said, prompting Charlotte to dig further in the package. Charlotte put her hand over her mouth when she found the second gift, and Gran smiled. "I bought that little bungalow on the beach when I first found you and your mom, and I kept it in case the two of you ever needed a home. It's been rented all these years, but it's yours now, along with all the rent money I've collected. You can keep it and use the rent money to fix it up or sell it and buy yourself a fancy house somewhere. Either way you'll have enough to start your future without having to settle for anything less than what your heart says is right."

Charlotte threw herself in her gran's arms and sobbed like she hadn't cried in years. "You'll be here to guide me, Gran," she said with a sniffle. "Nothing will ever come between us."

On Sunday Gran drove back to Martinsville, and Ryan drove Charlotte, her mom, and Becca back to the airport. It had been an amazing weekend and one that Charlotte would never forget. Becca had met Jared and had spent most of Saturday night on the phone with him. Gran had given her a home on the beach, and she hadn't even had a chance to tell Ryan of it yet. But the best part was having all the special people in her life together to share in her graduation.

On the ride back to Bloomington she laid her head back and thought about all her dreams as a girl, what she'd thought college would be like and her plans for the future, when one recurring theme started to play in her head. Nick. He was always supposed to have been a part of this, and her heart ached at the revelation. Looking over at Ryan, she felt almost as if she were cheating on him, and he didn't deserve that.

118

Ryan had been nothing but loving and supportive, so how could she be letting thoughts of Nick Greyson mess with her mind again?

Chapter 44

Now

"What are your plans for the Fourth of July?" Carol asked Charlotte on Thursday afternoon. "You do remember Monday is a holiday, right?"

Trying not to make eye contact with her assistant, Charlotte fibbed, "Of course I remember, Carol. No one forgets our country's Independence Day!"

Carol laughed. "You did forget!"

Charlotte began mentally looking at the calendar, and crap, the holiday was Monday, and she had no plans at all. Last year she and Peter had gone to a concert in Bradenton and watched the fireworks from the harbor restaurant on the Manatee River. While it had been nice, it had been nothing like the celebrations she had been a part of with her friends as kid. Closing her eyes, she could almost smell marshmallows roasting over the pit at the marina and see the names written with sparklers at the water's edge on the beach. Nick, Becca, Noah, and even Maya had been part of the festivities, and for just a moment she was transported back to those magical times.

"Boss, can you hear me?" Carol asked. "Earth to Charlotte; come in, Charlotte."

Snapping her head in Carol's direction, Charlotte sighed. "Just remembering the good old days," she said with a smile. "How about you? Any special date for the long weekend?"

"If only," Carol replied with a sigh of her own. "Other than the Greyson brothers it seems like Anna Maria is fresh out of hot-blooded males. Hey, maybe you could put in a good word for me with Nick? Noah and I had some fun when we went out before, but he had to leave for a big fishing tournament, and that was the last I heard from him."

Charlotte really liked Carol, but her assistant was very aggressive where men were concerned, and she wasn't about to push her on Noah. Besides, she was just getting her friendship reestablished with the Greyson family, and she wasn't about to do anything to jeopardize that.

"I've never known you to need help getting a man's attention, Carol," Charlotte teased. Before the conversation went any further, she was saved by the ringing of the phone. She reached for the receiver, and Carol headed back to her desk.

"This is Charlotte Luce. May I help you?" she said into the phone.

"I certainly hope so," answered a very sexy voice.

Heat spread over every inch of Charlotte's body. She responded as seductively as possible, "At Olde Florida Bank we pride ourselves in satisfying our customers' needs, so please tell me what I can do." *Shit, shit, shit, did I just say that?* she silently asked herself.

Evidently Nick was caught off guard as much she was, because it took him a few seconds to say anything. "Um, I have some errands to run in the morning, so I just wanted to confirm tomorrow night. I'll pick you up at five thirty. Dress casually and comfortably. And, Charlotte, as you've pointed out before, I'm not a customer of Olde Florida's, but I do appreciate your eagerness to keep me satisfied." Before she could say another word, he hung up.

Charlotte needed a cold shower and a glass of wine, but since it was just three thirty she had to make do with the large Diet Coke she had sitting on her desk and a quick call to Becca.

Friday morning Charlotte got up extra early so she could wash and dry her shoulder-length curls. She already felt guilty about cutting out of work early, so she knew there wouldn't be time to wash, condition, and work some Nick Chavez Mesquite Hair Serum magic into her hair and still be ready by five thirty. Deciding to try something new, she popped a Kauai dark-roast coffee pod into her Keurig and pulled out the carton of coconut-flavored creamer she had bought the night before instead of an Almond Joy bar. Life was about compromise, right?

An hour later her hair routine was complete, and she was ready to get dressed. *TGIF,* she thought, pulling on jeans and a red Olde Florida Bank shirt. Thankfully Carol's reminder about the upcoming holiday had come soon enough that Charlotte had time to suggest patriotic colors to the staff for dress-down day. Putting a white scarf around her hair, she felt very *Yankee Doodle Dandy*! She kissed her fingertips, touched Gran's locket, and headed out into the brilliant Florida sunshine.

By three thirty Charlotte had returned every customer call, cleaned out her e-mail, and even taken a great loan application, and she was starting to get nervous as hell. She and Becca had talked for almost an hour the night before, and she'd thought she was in control of her emotions. But all of a sudden it hit her, this was her first real date with Nick. Sure, they had gone out together lots of times when they were kids, but he had specifically called this a date, and that made it different. Finally, at four o'clock she couldn't stand it anymore, so she closed down her computer, went out to wish the staff a safe and fun Fourth of July weekend, and headed home.

Just as she was getting ready to step in the shower, her cell phone rang, and Charlotte panicked. What if it was Nick calling to cancel their date? She hit the accept button cautiously and was pleasantly surprised to hear her mom's voice. "Hi, Mom," she answered, "what's going on?"

Maggie had been living in an artists' colony in Arizona since right after Charlotte left for college and had become successful selling her handmade jewelry there. She and Charlotte usually talked every couple of weeks but always on a Sunday, never during the week.

"I thought you might be going to Becca's for the long weekend," her mom exclaimed, "but I needed you to be the first to know. Thomas and I are engaged, Lottie. We're getting married!"

Charlotte was in shock. Love-'em-and-leave-'em Maggie Luce was getting married? Charlotte sat down on her bed before responding.

"I'm so happy for you, Mom, but also in a state of disbelief. You just mentioned Thomas to me last month, and now you're engaged?"

Maggie giggled like a schoolgirl, and Charlotte could hear the love in her voice. "I never expected this to happen," she said gently, "but I haven't been this happy in a long, long time."

"I'm happy for you, Mom," Charlotte told her, and she really was. Her mom deserved someone special, and Charlotte knew Thomas had to be for her mom to have agreed to marry him. "When do I get to meet your new fiancé, and when is the wedding?"

"Well," Maggie said, "I was hoping you might take some vacation time and come to Arizona in October? We wanted to get married right away, but Thomas's son, Chad, is in the marines, and he can't get leave until then. We really want you and Chad to stand up with us."

"I'm sure I can work something out. Why don't you send me the dates you want me there, and I'll get it on the calendar? I really am happy for you, Mom. I hate to have to hang up, but I have a date at five thirty and still need to shower and dress."

"Where's Peter taking you, honey?" Maggie asked.

Shit, shit, shit! Charlotte realized she hadn't told her mom she and Peter had broken up. "Um, I'm not going out with Peter. Actually, I have a date with Nick." Charlotte could hear the thoughts tumbling around in her mother's head.

"Nick Greyson?" her mom asked guardedly. "I didn't know he was back in town. And what happened to Peter?"

"Mom, I truly don't have time to tell you everything right now, but yes, my date is with Nick Greyson, and Peter and I aren't seeing each other anymore. I'll call you tomorrow, and we'll have a real conversation, but I have to go. I love you, Mom, and congratulations." Charlotte ended the call before her mom could say another word, put her phone on vibrate, and headed to the shower. All the anxiety she had been feeling was now tripled, and Nick would be there in less than forty minutes.

With her legs shaved and her body exfoliated and covered with Victoria Secret's coconut oil, her new favorite flavor, she was just getting into her clothes at five fifteen. Deciding that casual and comfortable allowed for pants, she put on a pair of white ankle-length trousers and a coral silk blouse. Slipping on a pair of strappy white sandals and adding another swipe of coral lip gloss, she was finished just as the doorbell rang.

As always, her locket was the last thing she put on, and she asked Gran for extra guidance for the evening ahead. Grabbing her purse, she opened the door to her bungalow, and sweet mother, Nick took her breath away. Dressed in dark-washed jeans and a light-blue, button-down shirt with the sleeves rolled up, he looked as if he'd just stepped off an ad for hot, sexy male! The blue of his shirt brought out the blue of his eyes, and Charlotte felt as if she needed another shower after just one look at him. There wasn't an inch of her body that wasn't on fire, and some of her body parts felt as if they had already been doused with water. This was not the way she wanted this evening to begin.

"Hi" was all Charlotte could get out of her dry, parched mouth.

"Hi, yourself," Nick said with a wink, obviously aware of her reaction to him. "Are you ready to go?"

Charlotte couldn't get any words out, so she just nodded her response. Nick took her hand and smiled, his face lighting up when he looked at her. He whispered in her ear, "You look beautiful, and I'm starting to feel the satisfaction already." If he hadn't been holding her hand, she would have melted right there on her front step.

For a few moments they rode in silence, and then out of the blue Charlotte blurted out, "My mom's getting married."

Nick was well aware of Maggie Luce's reputation in Anna Maria, as well as her long-standing aversion to marriage. "And how do you feel about that?" he asked.

Charlotte shrugged. "I'm not really sure," she said. "I knew she was seeing this man, Thomas, but after all these years, I guess I never expected her to have a serious relationship. I mean, I want her to be happy; it's just kind of a shock."

Nick reached for her hand and smiled. "I've always wished that my dad would find someone and get over his obsession with my mom, but I do admit, it would seem weird if he actually started seeing someone after all this time."

124

"She just told me all of this right before you arrived, but from what I understand, they're getting married in Arizona this fall. Something about his son being on leave from the marines."

The expression on Charlotte's face showed that she wasn't nearly as okay with her mom's news as she was pretending to be, so Nick quickly changed the subject. "So how was your day? Anything exciting in the world of high finance?"

"Busy as usual for a Friday, and of course with the bank being closed on Monday there was extra lobby traffic. That reminds me—how are you coming with your dad's situation?"

Nick let go of her hand and cleared his throat. "Um, it appears that the deficit has something to do with Dad loaning Maya and Dimitri money to buy Dimitri's family's restaurant and then them not putting it back against his line of credit when they made payments. He's really embarrassed about it and doesn't want them to know, so we're all kind of acting like it didn't happen."

The explanation didn't feel quite right to Charlotte, but what had happened wasn't really any of her business. The bank had been paid, and no loss had occurred, so she decided not to say anything. "I'm just glad it's behind you," she said, but Nick only nodded.

"Tell me about Stavros," Charlotte said. "I read about it in the newspaper, but I didn't realize that Maya was married to Dimitri Maris. The restaurant critic who wrote the article said it was one of the ten hidden gems in Florida. That's quite a compliment!"

Nick's smile was enough to tell Charlotte how proud of his sister and brother-in-law he was. "The restaurant was in trouble before Dimi and Maya bought it from his parents, but they've done an amazing job of revitalizing it. Tarpon Springs is still a quaint Greek fishing village, but like everything it needed some new blood to get it moving again. Dimi is an authentic Greek chef, and with Maya's marketing background they've really taken it to the next level. I can't wait for you to meet Dimi and see Maya again."

Charlotte sat back and thought about the last time she and Nick had been to Tarpon Springs together. For her fifteenth birthday Nick had borrowed his dad's truck and taken her on an adventure. They'd done the sponge boat tour where the diver "just happened" to find a sponge; had a picnic lunch of Kalamata olives, cheese, and fresh bread on the dock; and then wandered through the shops, where Nick had bought her a coral ring with a silver braided band. She had treasured that ring and worn it every day until the night of the senior send-off. Looking down at her coral blouse, she wondered what Nick would have said if she had worn it tonight. Would he have even remembered it? She still had the ring; it was locked in a box along with the emerald bracelet Ryan had given her for her college graduation. *Kind of like my vault of missed opportunities of love,* she thought.

Chapter 45

Then

Soon after graduation Charlotte moved all her things from the dorm into an apartment in Indianapolis that she was sharing with Cristi and Ellen. She already had a job lined up with a major accounting firm in the city, and living with her two good friends again seemed heaven-sent. Ryan had hoped she would stay in Bloomington so she would be closer to him, but as always, he was understanding and accepted her need for some independence.

After an exciting, and grueling, year of working part-time and attending class full-time to earn her MBA, Charlotte was ready for a break when Ryan invited her to spend the weekend with him in Bloomington. Because of her hectic schedule he had come to Indianapolis to see her most of the time, but she had four days off work and class, and a getaway with Ryan sounded perfect. He even offered to come to Indy to pick her up so she could relax, but she assured him the drive would do her good.

It was a beautiful Friday afternoon as Charlotte got in her car and headed south to Bloomington. She and Ryan hadn't had a whole weekend alone since Christmas, and she was so looking forward to it. As she drove with both hands on the steering wheel, the sunlight hit her emerald bracelet, and she wondered again what she had done to deserve such a wonderful guy. Ryan was patient and kind, not to mention gorgeous, and she smiled as she thought about all the fun they could have with two entire days together.

Pulling into Ryan's driveway, Charlotte thought about her little bungalow on the beach back in Anna Maria. She had never really thought about going back to Florida. Her mom wasn't there, and Gran and Ryan were here in Indiana. But she hadn't been able to bring herself to sell the cottage that her gran had so lovingly kept for her all these years either. Maybe it was just knowing that she had a home if she ever needed one, or maybe it was Gran; she wasn't sure. Somehow, though, whenever she thought about her "forever" place, it wasn't the lovely house standing before her now but a little pink-and-white vision that came to mind.

Ryan opened the door before she had a chance to knock and pulled her in for a long, hot kiss. "I've really missed you this week," he said with longing, and he wrapped her in his arms for another long, delicious kiss.

"Is this how you greet all your guests?" Charlotte teased.

With a light slap to her bottom Ryan picked her up and headed up the stairs. "Only the ones I plan to ravish," he declared. By the time they reached the bedroom, Charlotte's giggles had turned to moans.

It was dark outside when Charlotte woke up alone in Ryan's bed. Wonderful aromas were coming from downstairs, and her mouth watered as she remembered she had skipped lunch in her hurry to get away. She splashed water on her face in the bathroom and put her hair up into a ponytail before slipping into a pair of shorts and a T-shirt. Not exactly a femme fatale, but she knew Ryan wasn't expecting one.

Quietly walking into the kitchen, Charlotte watched Ryan cook for her and got butterflies just admiring his handsome physique in a pair of old sweats and a T-shirt, chopping vegetables and humming.

"Hey, beautiful," he said when he saw her, "did you have a nice nap? I do have to say I hope that you were sleepy because I wore you out and not because you found my lovemaking boring," he smirked as he came around to kiss her. Charlotte blushed, which brought a huge smile to his face.

"How about a glass of wine? I have chicken in the oven, a Caesar salad in the fridge, and vegetables ready to throw on the grill." Ryan stopped long enough to pour her a glass of pinot grigio and then continued, "And then I thought we'd have dessert upstairs." He gave Charlotte a look with so much heat that she felt it across the room, and of course, she blushed again.

Chapter 46

Then

Saturday morning was dark and stormy, but unlike yesterday afternoon Ryan was very much with her, snuggled against her back with his arm possessively wrapped around her. Pulling the covers up tighter, she went back into a deep sleep. She dreamed of white sand and teal water. When she woke up again, her heart was pounding, and she could hear Ryan in the shower. *Where did that come from?* she wondered. She rarely thought of Florida anymore unless she was talking to Becca, but now it felt like it was really on her mind.

Ryan stepped out of the bathroom and gave her that heart-melting smile of his. Last night had been great, better than great, and she was happy knowing that Ryan was happy. In the eighteen months that they had been together, Charlotte had often struggled to relax during sex, and Ryan felt very responsible. Charlotte tried to tell him that it was her and not him, but since she had never been with another man, he wouldn't accept it. She was also a little reluctant to try new things, but last night had been really good for both of them, and she hoped they had turned a corner.

"You look like the cat that ate the canary, Miss Luce," Ryan teased her. "What's going on in that pretty head of yours this morning?"

Charlotte's mind was reeling. She was dreaming about Anna Maria Island, and Ryan thought she was thinking about sex! *How do I get out of this mess?* she asked herself. Finally, she smiled shyly and said, "A girl has to have a few secrets, now doesn't she? So why don't you go make us some coffee, and I'll shower and dress and then be all yours for the rest of the day."

"I'm counting on that," Ryan replied as he headed down the stairs.

Charlotte was not a big breakfast eater, so when she got downstairs, Ryan had coffee and fruit waiting for her. It was perfect, and it meant a lot that he understood her issues with food. He fixed himself a bagel with cream cheese to go with the fruit, and he left the bagels and cream cheese out if she wanted some. He never tried to force her to eat or to change her habits for him.

"Let's take our food into the den," Ryan suggested. "I'd love to go out on the deck, but it's still raining, and the den is cozy. Anyway, I have something I want to talk to you about."

Shit, shit, shit! Was talking ever a good thing?

Ryan sat down on the oversize leather sofa and patted the seat beside him. Trying to act casual, Charlotte sat down and pulled her feet underneath her. She nonchalantly popped a piece of strawberry in her mouth, but her heart was racing. Absentmindedly she reached up and touched her locket, as if willing Gran's presence to bring her strength.

Sensing her discomfort, Ryan took her hands in his and smiled at her as if she were the only woman on earth. Normally that smile made Charlotte feel warm all over, but for some reason the butterflies in her stomach this time were not the good kind.

"Charlotte," Ryan began, "I've been offered a job. It's a really good job with the company I've always wanted to work for, and I'm pretty excited about it." Still holding on to her hands, he looked up to gauge her reaction before going on. "It's on Wall Street, in New York City."

She knew she needed to say something. Ryan was looking at her with such emotion in his eyes, but she was afraid if she opened her mouth she would start to cry. Taking a few seconds to get her thoughts together, Charlotte replied softly, "I'm really happy for you, Ryan. This is a great opportunity, and if it's where you've always wanted to work, it's like a dream come true."

"It's a great opportunity for *us*, Charlotte," he responded with enthusiasm. "*You* are my dream come true, and taking you to New York will just be icing on the cake! You're going to love it there just as much as I do."

Shut the front door! Was he asking her to go to New York with him? The butterflies in her stomach had just turned into big old bats, and they were threatening to fly north! Charlotte put her head in her hands and tried to stay calm.

"I still have a year left on my master's program," she explained. "I can't go to New York."

"There are great schools in New York, and with your GPA you'll be able to transfer to one of them easily."

"But what about my job and…?"

Ryan lifted her chin so she was looking at him. "There are jobs in New York too, plus Broadway and Central Park and shopping and nightlife, and I can't wait to show it all to you." He looked like a child on Christmas morning, and more than anything she didn't want to spoil this for him.

"But I don't think I can afford to live in New York City and still go to school. I can only do it in Indianapolis because of Cristi and Ellen." How could he not understand?

"You could always live with me," Ryan said, and Charlotte could read the hope in his eyes, even though she had told him before it was something she wasn't comfortable with.

"But what about Gran?" she asked.

Ryan ran his fingers through his hair and then looked right at her, his beautiful violet-gray eyes filled with sadness as they implored her to give him a chance. "I would marry you tomorrow, Charlotte, if I thought it would make a difference. I love you. You're everything I've ever wanted in a woman, but I've always felt part of you was holding back. We, you, can't move forward if you can't let go of the past, and I think that's what the problem is. Can you tell me I'm wrong?"

No longer able to hold back the tears, Charlotte wrapped her arms around her knees and rocked back and forth. She wanted to be able to give her whole heart to Ryan, but she knew that a part of it wasn't hers to give. She didn't want to lose him either, but she knew she couldn't go to New York.

"Are you breaking up with me?" she sobbed.

As always Ryan was the perfect gentleman. He put his arms around her and pulled her close. "I've already accepted the job, Charlotte, and obviously I was hoping for a different outcome today. I'm putting my house on the market on Monday, but I'll be working in Bloomington until the end of the month. That gives you a few weeks to think about everything we've talked about. I meant every word I said, and I want nothing more than to have a wonderful adventure with you. But to answer your question, I'm pretty sure it's you who is breaking up with me."

The wonderful weekend they had planned was slipping away, and there was nothing Charlotte could do to stop it. They watched whatever was on TV, sitting in chairs instead of together on the couch, and at dinnertime Ryan announced he was ordering a pizza. That in itself was a big deal because Ryan had always loved cooking for her, but she was fine with pizza. After all, nothing was more comforting to someone with an obsession with food than carbs covered in greasy cheese.

About eleven o'clock Charlotte said she was tired and was going up to bed. Ryan just said good night and let her go up alone. Around midnight she felt him slip under the covers, but instead of reaching for her, he turned away. They had never before shared a bed and not made love, and Charlotte realized this was really the beginning to the end. She willed herself not to cry, and after an hour or two she finally drifted into a restless sleep.

It was still dark when Charlotte woke up at four thirty on Sunday morning, but she knew right away that Ryan was no longer in bed. She smelled coffee being brewed so she knew he was awake too. Without even bothering to shower, she put on a pair of jeans and a sweatshirt, did a quick freshen up in the bathroom, and threw the rest of her things in her bag. Looking around the room, she felt a huge lump in her throat as she replayed all the memories of this room through her mind—The night she had lost her virginity, when Ryan had first told her he loved her, the spooning after sex—every one of them special until last night.

She just hoped that wouldn't be the memory of her Ryan would take with him to New York.

When she got downstairs, Ryan was sitting at the island drinking coffee from the mug she had gotten for him right after they had decided to be exclusive. The words on the front read, "**OFF the MARKET**. With Ryan being the current most eligible bachelor in Indiana and a stockbroker, she had loved its double meaning. "Hi," she said quietly, not sure how to approach him.

"Hi, yourself," he answered with a wary smile. Charlotte could see the hurt and the uncertainty in his eyes, and it was killing her inside. Ryan was every girl's fantasy, so why couldn't she just give him what he wanted?

The plan had been for Charlotte to stay until Monday morning and then head back to Indy when Ryan left for work, but she knew staying there was only going to make things harder. "I'm going to head out," she said as casually as possible, "hopefully get a start before the traffic gets bad." Inside she hoped he would ask her to stay so they could work things out, but instead he just nodded. When she got to the front door, she thought her knees would buckle, but she held on to the doorframe and turned to look once more at his beautiful face. "Will you call me?" she asked, trying not to sound pathetic.

"I'm flying to New York on Friday to look for an apartment, but I'll call you when I get back on Sunday evening." A whole week without talking to each other? They had never gone more than a day without a call before. All of a sudden, the finality hit her. Couldn't she just suck it up and be the girlfriend Ryan deserved? The answer was no. Pretending wasn't the answer, and it wasn't what Ryan would want. Right now it seemed so much easier, though.

Ryan put his arms around her and held her for a minute and then gave her a soft kiss before pulling away. "You are an amazing woman, Charlotte Luce. Don't ever doubt that. And no matter what happens, know that I truly love you and want nothing but happiness for you."

All Charlotte could get out of her mouth was "I'll talk to you on Sunday," and then she got into her car and sped away. At the first exit she pulled into a McDonald's and ordered the hotcake breakfast with extra syrup. She needed comfort in the worst way, and nothing gave comfort like Mickey D's. She gobbled down her food and then placed a call while still in the parking lot.

"Hello," answered an obviously still-asleep Becca. "What's wrong that you're calling me at this time of day, Lottie?"

"I'm pretty sure Ryan and I just broke up," Charlotte got out between sobs. She waited for the support from her best friend, the one who had been there for her the last time she'd had a major heartbreak, forgetting that Becca was a newlywed, married to Ryan's fraternity brother Dr. Jared Tyler.

"Ryan broke up with you?" Becca asked in the same voice she would use to ask if Charlotte needed air to breathe. Becca knew how crazy Ryan was about Charlotte, so something wasn't adding up.

"Not exactly," Charlotte faltered. "He said I was breaking up with him."

"Oh, Lottie," Becca moaned, "what did you do?"

Chapter 47

Now

The rest of the ride to Tarpon Springs was spent with small talk, and before Charlotte knew it, they arrived at the restaurant. The outside of Stavros was beautiful, and Charlotte thought it looked like it really belonged in Greece. She was still admiring the old-world charm when Nick took her arm and ushered her inside.

When she spotted Nick's big sister—well, older sister to be exact, as she was petite compared to Nick—her insides started to churn, and all of a sudden she couldn't breathe. Just because the men in the Greyson family still cared about her didn't mean Maya would welcome her with open arms. But to Charlotte's amazement, that's just what Maya did.

"Lottie, let me get a good look at you," Maya cried after releasing her from a big hug. "You are absolutely gorgeous! You were always such a pretty girl. I just knew you would be a stunning woman."

Me, stunning? Charlotte thought. She looked up at Nick, and he tilted his head and smiled as if to say, *See, I told you so.* Charlotte's cheeks turned a pretty shade of pink at the compliment, but she smiled at Maya and thanked her for the lovely words. Maya grabbed her for another sisterly hug and introduced her to the man who was now standing beside her.

"Lottie, this is my husband and partner in crime, Dimitri Maras. Dimi, Lottie is Nick's childhood girlfriend and the sister we never had."

Childhood girlfriend? Sister? Charlotte's head was spinning, and she was at a total loss for words. Did Maya remember things differently than she did, or was she just razzing Nick? Charlotte had seen Noah do it a lot over the past few weeks but had never expected it from Maya.

Before she could say anything, Dimitri spoke up. "Wow," he said to Nick, "why did you ever let this one get away? She's way hotter than the last girl you brought here."

"Okay, you two," Nick growled, "enough. Don't make me wish that I'd taken Charlotte to a good restaurant. I thought you could use the business."

Charlotte looked around at the full tables and people waiting to get seats and knew they were all just having fun with each other. She smiled at Dimitri. "It's nice to meet you, Dimitri. Nick has said nothing but great things about you and your restaurant, but I would love to know more about the last girl that he brought here," she said sweetly. *There,* she thought, *I can play too!*

Dimitri and Maya laughed, but Nick didn't crack a smile. "Oh, I like this one, Nick," Dimitri said. "I can tell she's a handful."

Nick shook his head and looked right at Charlotte. "That she is, brother-in-law, but I'm working on it."

Holy shit, Charlotte thought. *What does that mean?*

With that Dimitri excused himself to get back to the kitchen, and Maya took them to their table, which was situated in a small alcove with a wonderful view of the water—very private and very romantic. Maya lit the candle on the table and told them Dimitri had prepared a special meal for them and that she would be right back with a bottle of wine.

Nick reached over and took her hands in his, a gesture Charlotte was beginning to enjoy. "Well, what do you think so far? I know Maya was really looking forward to seeing you again, so I hope you weren't too embarrassed by their antics. And just to set the record straight, I've never brought another woman here; you are the first."

Charlotte felt warm all over and couldn't wait for a glass of wine. She was actually on a date with Nick. Every woman in the place was secretly looking at him, but he was with her and looking at her as if she were something on the menu. The warm feeling in her stomach became an inferno a little farther south.

Maya returned with two kinds of wine and poured a small amount of each for Nick to sample. "This is Athiri," she said. "Can you taste the nectarines? If you like a crisp white, it's one of my favorites. The next is Xinomavro, and it's a lovely spicy red."

Nick tried both wines and offered them for Charlotte to sample as well.

"I'm going to leave it to you and Maya to make the decision," she said. "I'm sure I'll like either one."

"Let's go with the Xinomavro," Nick told his sister. "I like spicy, and I like red." He winked at Charlotte, and she felt as if he were talking about her and not the wine. Hoping to combat her nerves, she took a huge gulp of the wine Maya had set before her. Unfortunately, the warmth of the wine only added to the heat between her legs, and she knew she was a goner.

Dinner was amazing, but there was way more food than Charlotte could even begin to eat. Dimitri had prepared two of his specialties for them—Kufta, which was seasoned ground beef served with grilled vegetables, pineapple, and tzatziki sauce, and Shish Taouk chicken, which was marinated in yogurt and tarragon curry and then grilled and topped with garlic sauce. Alongside was a delicious couscous and an avocado salad and of course, freshly made pitas.

Charlotte looked at the massive amounts of food and felt as if she had gained five pounds already. There was no way that she wasn't going to enjoy this dinner, though, so she made up her mind to at least taste everything and then run through the botanical gardens twice in the morning.

Nick was just finishing up the last of the chicken—*where did that man put it all?*—when Maya stopped back at their table. "How was it?" she asked brightly. "My husband is the best Greek chef in the country, but I always like an unbiased opinion."

Nick and Charlotte both laughed, and then Charlotte said in all seriousness, "It was beyond words, Maya. The flavors and presentation were out of this world, and I can't thank you and Dimitri enough for honoring us with such a divine meal."

The glow on Maya's face said it all, but Charlotte was not prepared for what she said next. "So, you're coming to the party at the marina tomorrow, right? We're bringing the girls for the holiday weekend, and I can't wait for you to meet them."

Charlotte sat there dumbfounded, not sure what to say. Once again Nick jumped in to save her. "I was going to ask her on the ride home, but since you've already let the cat out of the bag, I'll do it now. Charlotte, I would love for you to join my family tomorrow for our annual Fourth of July weekend bash. Will you come?"

Shit, shit, shit! This was awkward. What if Nick was just asking her because Maya had told her about the party? Yes, she had always been included when they were kids, but this was different. Waging a war in her head about how to answer, she almost missed what Nick said next.

"I really want you to be there," he said hopefully. "Will you be my date?"

She knew she wouldn't be able to speak, so she nodded her acceptance. Then her first thought was, *What bathing suit will I wear?*

Nick settled the bill and led her out to his Jeep. It was a beautiful Florida night with millions of stars twinkling in the sky. As they drove, Nick reached over and put his hand on her knee. Oh crap! What did that mean? Charlotte closed her eyes to think about the situation, and within moments she was sound asleep. Too much wine and rich food had taken its toll on her, and she slept all the way back to Anna Maria Island.

Chapter 48

Then

Charlotte was miserable. She and Becca had had their first fight ever, and it was killing her. When she had told Becca about Ryan's surprise plans to move to New York and how he had more or less assumed she would want to go with him, Becca's response had been "Crap, I knew it was a bad idea!"

"You knew about all of this, and you didn't warn me?" Charlotte had cried in response. "Why?"

"I wanted to tell you, really I did, but I only knew because Ryan told Jared, and Jared said it wasn't our place to interfere. I told Jared how much you hated surprises and that you weren't going to be okay with going to New York, but, Lottie, he's my husband. Please try to understand." By that point Becca had been crying too, but it hadn't stopped Charlotte from throwing out a cheap shot.

"And I'm your best friend," she had responded coldly.

The conversation hadn't gotten any better, so they'd hung up, and now Charlotte was truly alone. Cristi and Ellen would never understand her decision, as they thought the moon hung on Ryan Noble, and Gran was in California with Charlotte's uncle and two cousins. That only left her mom, and Charlotte didn't want to go there. She loved her mom, but after the issue with Nick she knew it was better to keep her love life to herself.

Sunday afternoon dragged on forever, and when bedtime finally came, Charlotte found that she couldn't sleep. Her heart ached at the thought of losing Ryan, but her soul ached at the thought of losing Becca. She didn't know how to fix things, though. After tossing and turning for most of the night, she got up around five and started a pot of coffee.

She was on her third cup when her cell phone rang and the name Jared Tyler popped up on the screen. Thinking it was Becca, she answered with a joyful "Hello!" only to be disappointed—at least momentarily.

A masculine voice chuckled on the other end. "I take it from that warm greeting you were expecting this call to be from my wife, am I right?"

Charlotte sighed and tried to be cordial to Jared, but truth be told, she was mad at him. *What right did he have telling Becca that she couldn't tell me about Ryan's secret?*

"Charlotte, I called to apologize for not listening to Becca when she warned me you wouldn't like Ryan's surprise and for pulling the husband card out when she wanted to get involved. She's really unhappy with me, so much so that she locked me out of our bedroom last night. And, well, you know we've only been married a few weeks, so it was really hard."

Charlotte found herself smiling for the first time since Friday. If Becca had locked Jared out of their bedroom, she must have been really pissed, because from what Becca had shared with her, there was magic happening in that room every night. And usually every morning too!

"It's okay, Jared," she told him. "I'm so used to having Becca to myself that sometimes I forget she has more in her life than just me. That was really selfish of me; I know. I promise I'll talk with Becca this morning, and you'll be back in your bed tonight."

She could hear the relief in his voice as he said, "Thanks, Charlotte, that means a lot. But I want you to know that you haven't lost Becca as a friend; you've gained me as one too. We both were hoping things would work out with you and Ryan, but we want you to be happy, whether that's with or without Ryan."

His kind words brought the tears back to her eyes, but now she knew that she wasn't alone, and she had also caught a glimpse of what true love really looked like.

Chapter 49

Now

"Hey, sleepyhead, we're home," Nick said gently as he tried to wake Charlotte up. He knew it was his own fault that she fell asleep since he'd had only one glass of wine, and she had finished off the bottle. Being in law enforcement, he understood the dangers of drinking and driving, so he was always careful whenever he was behind the wheel.

Charlotte opened her eyes, looked up at Nick, and closed them again. *Crap! Did I really fall asleep on my first real date with Nick Greyson?* She was mortified and opened her eyes just enough to try to gauge how he was reacting. To her surprise, he was smiling.

"You're really cute when you sleep," he teased, "although I would never have pegged you as a snorer."

Charlotte sat up straight, all ready to defend herself, but realized he was laughing. "I do not snore, Mr. Greyson," she said, pretending to be offended, "but I have been told that I talk in my sleep. I hope I didn't say anything incriminating." She batted her eyelashes like a true femme fatale but almost choked on what Nick said next.

"Well, you did say that you hoped I would kiss you, although I was hoping you were awake when you said it." He gave her a look so hot and smoldering that it took every ounce of strength she had not to throw her arms around his neck and bring him in for a big one, but thankfully Nick took care of that for her.

Charlotte had waited over half of her life for a kiss from Nick, and when it finally happened, he didn't disappoint. His lips started out soft and warm, with a slight nibble on her bottom lip, and when she opened her mouth to moan, he went in for the kill, taking her face in his hands. Charlotte thought she had met some good kissers in the past, but compared to Nick, those other guys were amateurs. Finally, he pulled back long enough to look into her eyes. Charlotte would have agreed to anything at that moment. She could definitely see lust in his eyes, so when he said, "It was a perfect evening, Charlotte. I'll pick you up at ten in the morning," she knew he was putting on the brakes.

Walking up the steps to her cottage, Charlotte wasn't sure if she was mad at Nick for being such a gentleman or happy he hadn't taken advantage of the situation. One way or another she knew she would be thinking about that kiss well into the night, because even if it was almost midnight, she knew she had to call Becca!

Chapter 50

Then

Charlotte waited by the phone all day on Sunday, but true to his word Ryan didn't call until late in the afternoon. Trying to act as if everything was normal, she asked about his week but was met with a two-word answer: "Long and tiring."

With tears welling up in her eyes, Charlotte took a stab at making things better. "I've thought a lot about our conversation, Ryan. I don't understand why we can't have a long-distance relationship while I finish school, and then in a year we can reevaluate things." There, wasn't that a compromise?

Ryan was quite for a few seconds, and then he sighed. "I love you, Charlotte. Can you honestly say that you love me in return?"

"You know that I do," she cried.

"Then say it," he demanded, throwing her a curve.

That was when Charlotte understood that it was really over.

"You can't, can you?" he said softly. "Which is why waiting isn't going to make things better. I know you haven't experienced life the way I have, and I'd be willing to wait for you if I knew that you loved me, but you don't, at least not the way I love you. Prolonging the inevitable isn't going to make it any easier.

"The good news is," he continued, "I got a full-price offer on my house this week, and I've signed a lease on an apartment, so it looks like I'll be heading to New York a little sooner than I planned."

Charlotte could hardly get the words out she was crying so hard. "Please don't hate me, Ryan," she sobbed. "I do care for you. It's just…"

"It's just that I'm not him, right? I need to go, Charlotte. I'm exhausted, and I have a lot to do in the next week. If you need me, you know you can always call."

Charlotte held on to the receiver, listening to the dial tone, as the irony hit her. Nick had broken her heart, and because of him she had broken Ryan's. Love was just fucked up, and at that moment, she didn't want to ever have anything more to do with it.

Chapter 51

Now

Charlotte had every intention of getting up early and doubling her Saturday-morning run, but when the alarm started to beep, she turned it off and snuggled back into her covers. Thinking about the upcoming party at the marina and the smoldering kiss Nick had given her the night before, she settled into deep sleep and didn't wake up until eight.

Shit, shit, shit, she thought, jumping out of bed and heading to her Keurig. Nick would be there in two hours, and she had so much to do. Putting a Starbucks cinnamon-latte pod in the pot, she decided after all the yummy food at last night's dinner, she needed to skip the cream and have her coffee black. Then she had an important decision to make: Which bathing suit would best show off her assets and still hold in her stomach?

She decided on a deep-purple one-piece with a bandeau top and a mock wraparound look. It was grown-up, without being too revealing. After all, Nick's ten-year-old twin nieces were going to be there, so she wanted to look like a lady. Besides, it had a matching long, flowy skirt cover-up that would be perfect for a long day on the water.

After washing and deep conditioning her hair, she wound strands around her fingers to give it that wavy beach look that she loved and slathered Victoria Secret's coconut oil all over her skin. She wasn't sure what had made Nick give her the superhot kiss the night before, but she wasn't going to jinx it by wearing a different fragrance today.

She just had time to fasten her locket around her neck and put on a little blush and lip gloss before she heard Nick's Jeep pull up in her drive. Should she answer the door right away, or should she make him wait? The thoughts going around in her head were daunting. Never good at playing games, she opened the door before he knocked and was pulled into the kiss of the century. Holy hell, that man knew how to make her melt!

"Hi," Charlotte said when she could catch her breath.

Nick smiled. "I haven't been able to stop thinking about you," he said, making her feel as if she had already had a dip in the gulf. He pulled her close and nibbled on her neck like she was on the breakfast menu.

Now she had two options. Pull him into her bedroom and have her way with him, or pull away and remind him that his family was waiting. She opted for the latter, although most of her body parts were not happy with the decision.

"Who all will be at the party today?" Charlotte asked, settling into her seat.

"Really just the family unless Noah brings a date. He doesn't usually bring his women around when the twins are there, so I imagine it will just be us. I can't wait for you to meet the girls," he added with a chuckle. "They are ten going on fifteen and really keep Maya and Dimi on their toes."

Charlotte hadn't heard a word after "just the family." There had been a time when she had felt like part of the Greyson family, but now? The dynamics had changed so much in the last few days. The last thing she wanted to do was overthink them, but where did she really fit in? Nick would be going back to work full-time now that he and Noah had figured out the situation with the marina's finances. Where did that leave her?

Feeling her car door open, Charlotte realized they had arrived at the marina. Nick was just about to bend down and kiss her when two identical mermaids wrapped their arms around his legs. "Uncle Nick!" they shouted. "Take us for a ride in the Jeep!"

Nick had always been good with younger kids when they were in school, but Charlotte was not at all prepared for the look of total devotion he gave his nieces. The girls were miniature versions of Maya, and it was very obvious they had all the men in the family wrapped around their fingers.

"Maybe later, ladies," he laughed, trying to dislodge them from his muscular thighs. "This is my friend Charlotte, and she's our guest today."

Charlotte couldn't help but grin at the sight of Nick trying to be firm with the two sandy-haired imps. She decided to help them all out. "Nonsense, Uncle Nick," she said with a smile. "These beauties want a ride in your Jeep, and a ride they shall have. I'll go inside and see if I can help Pop or maybe even say hello to Noah." She batted her eyelashes at him as she got out of the car, loving the growl he let out. Oh yeah, this was going to be a fun day.

Chapter 52

Then

Charlotte ripped open the mail and stared at her master's degree diploma. Finally, she could be done with school and focus on life. The accounting firm she worked for in Indianapolis had offered her a full-time job, and for the first time since her breakup with Ryan she was excited about the future. She had even had a date or two, but she knew in her heart a relationship was just not in the cards right now.

The last few months of school had been tough, and Charlotte knew she had neglected Gran, so to celebrate her final graduation she packed a bag and headed to Martinsville to surprise Gran for the weekend. But the surprise was on Charlotte, and it wasn't a good one.

The vibrant flowers that always stood proud and tall around the farmhouse were wilted and brown, and when Charlotte stepped into the kitchen, the place that always smelled of something fresh out of the oven, there was no smell at all.

"Gran?" she called, trying not to panic. "Are you here, Gran?" Gran would have told her if she was going to be out of town, so Charlotte started moving from room to room, searching for the grandmother she loved so much. She finally found Gran sleeping in her bed, covered with the quilt the two of them had made together when Charlotte was fourteen.

"Gran," she asked cautiously, "are you okay?" It was only eleven, and Gran never took naps, especially not in the morning.

"Lottie, is that you?" Gran asked, trying to sit up. "I was feeling so tired that I just needed to rest my eyes. What time is it?"

Charlotte knew this wasn't good, but she didn't want to show her concern, so she swallowed the lump in her throat and sat down on the bed. "As hard as you work around here, you're entitled to a nap every now and then," she said with a weak smile. "I came for the weekend, and you're going to take it easy and let me take care of you for a change. Okay?" Hoping against hope that Gran would get out of bed and say "Nonsense," Charlotte put her hands on her hips in a show of strength. Gran just nodded and lay back down.

Three months later, at only sixty-seven, Gran was gone. The doctor said her heart just gave out. She had never told Charlotte that she was suffering from congestive heart disease and had been adamant that no one else tell her either. All the excitement and the plans for the future meant nothing if she couldn't share them with Gran. The heartache she was feeling was like nothing she had ever experienced before.

The night before the funeral Becca and Jared flew in from New Smyrna Beach, and for the first time since Gran's death Charlotte allowed herself to cry. Becca held her while Jared wrapped his strong arms around both of their shoulders, gently patting and soothing the love of his life and her best friend.

"I should have been there more," Charlotte wept. "How could I have been so involved with my own life that I didn't stay in better contact?"

Becca pulled her in tighter, and Jared used his medical degree to try to ease her pain. "What was the one thing your gran wanted for your life, Lottie?" he asked. "Because you couldn't have changed the outcome of her disease. Yes, you could have quit going to school and work and stayed with her around the clock, but would that have made either of you happy or made the hurt any less today?"

Charlotte looked into his warm and caring eyes and shook her head. "Above all else Gran wanted me to experience the life my dad never had and to be thankful for each and every day. I know she

151

wouldn't want me to be sad, but I feel like a balloon that's had all the air let out. I need a focus to fill me up again."

Becca looked up at her husband and smiled, and he nodded his agreement. "Well, how about if we give you something good to focus on then? I'm pregnant, Lottie; Jared and I are going to have a baby."

This time both women were crying when Jared wrapped his arms around them, but they were tears of joy, with promise for the future.

That evening Becca pulled Charlotte aside with a strange message. "Do you remember my brother Brad?" Becca asked. "He sent me a text asking for you to call him tomorrow at the bank. He apologized for the timing but said he really needs to talk with you."

Brad was Becca's oldest sibling, and with ten years between them, he had never interacted with the girls much. "Do you think it has something to do with Gran's estate?" Charlotte asked. "She told me when she gave me the cottage on the beach that the farm would go to my uncle and his kids, and I can't see why she would have dealt with a bank in Florida when she's lived in Indiana her whole life. You don't think there's a problem with the cottage, do you? Gran transferred it to my name when I graduated from IU."

"My mom always said don't go borrowing trouble, so get through today, and you can call Brad tomorrow. Our flight doesn't leave until eight tomorrow night, so Jared and I will be here for moral support, okay?"

"I don't know what I would have done without you both, Becca. Mom wasn't comfortable being here with Gran's family, and without you, I would have been alone. I have to admit that I did think about calling Ryan, but I knew that wouldn't have been fair to him."

"Oh, sweetie," Becca said with a sigh, "Jared did call him. He would have come in a heartbeat, but we weren't sure it would have been fair to either of you. I'm sure you'll hear from him, though; Ryan thought the world of your gran. But sometimes it's better to just let sleeping dogs lie."

Charlotte nodded and grabbed her friend's hand, happy for her support and for her love.

152

Chapter 53

Now

When Nick came back from the ride with his nieces, he found Charlotte sitting on Noah's lap on the deck, wiggling and giggling while he tickled her unmercifully. "WTF, little brother?" Nick whispered in his ear. He was always conscious of his language when the girls were around but wanted to make his point. Charlotte was *his* date; Noah needed to get his hands off her!

He could see that Charlotte was blushing a shade somewhere between chianti and merlot, as she jumped up off of Noah's lap, but Noah just shrugged his shoulders. "Hey, you left her alone, and I was just keeping her entertained. Besides, I was curious if Lottie was still as ticklish as she used to be."

Nick was on the verge of a retort when Maya and Dimitri joined them on the deck. "What's all the commotion out here?" Maya asked. "If I didn't know better I would think my *baby* brothers were acting like teenagers instead of grown men."

Dimitri gave Charlotte a wink and pulled his wife in for a kiss. "Sometimes she forgets that she's not their mother," he teased. "You would think that once Their Royal Highnesses came along she would have given up on Mutt and Jeff."

Maya rolled her eyes but didn't pull away from her husband's embrace. "Speaking of the little goddesses, have you met our beautiful girls, Lottie?"

As if on cue, the two stepped out on the deck, one on each arm of their grandfather.

"Nikki, Steffi, I want to introduce you to Lottie Luce, an old friend of your uncle Nick's," Maya said with pride. "They met when they were just about your age."

"You don't look so old," one of the pint-size beauties said.

"Are you uncle Nick's girlfriend?" the other one asked.

Everyone except Nick was trying not to laugh as he ran his hand through his hair and knelt in front of them. "She's an old friend because we've known each other a really long time, and she is a girl and she is a friend. Let's just leave it at that, okay?"

The answer was enough to satisfy them, and in a shot they were off to torment Uncle Noah. "Take us for a Jet Ski ride, please!" they begged. And for the first time Charlotte witnessed Noah not being able to resist a female's plea. Sure enough, he grabbed a girl under each arm and headed off to the Jet Ski.

Pop went back into the house to work on lunch, and despite her requests to help, Charlotte was shooed out of the kitchen. "Go enjoy yourself, Lottie," he told her. "Just having you here today is a treat for me, and I want you kids to make a memory that will last a lifetime."

Charlotte knew he was being sincere, but she couldn't help but wonder about the meaning behind his words. Was this the last Fourth of July party the family would have or just the last one she would be invited to? Nick would be going back to his job full-time soon, as he really didn't have any reason to stay now. She couldn't think about that today, though. Today she wanted to be with her friends, and her adopted family, without worrying about tomorrow.

She was still lost in her thoughts when Maya took her hand and said, "Let's swim out to the pier. I haven't done that in years." She pulled her cover-up over her head, revealing the bathing suit Charlotte had borrowed when she had been there a few weeks before. Nick was looking at Maya in a way that she couldn't help but notice, so she asked,

154

"What are you staring at? Has it been that long since you've seen a woman in a bathing suit?"

"As a matter of fact not that long at all," Nick chuckled, "and one particular vision is burned in my brain." He looked at Charlotte with so much heat she thought for sure Dimitri would call him out on it, but Dimitri just smiled as Nick added, "It was a fine day for all of us."

Maya shook her head, oblivious to her brother's sense of humor, and dived into the crystal-blue water. Dimitri followed close behind, leaving Nick and Charlotte on the deck. When she untied her skirt, Charlotte looked up to see Nick staring at her. Her suit wasn't too revealing, so why did she feel so exposed?

"You take my breath away," he said softly, and Charlotte fell a little bit deeper under his spell.

Chapter 54

Now

If Charlotte had to use one word to describe the day at the marina with Nick's family, it would be *enchanted*. She loved getting to know Maya and Dimitri better, and even though Nikki and Steffi were ornery, the twins had already found a place in her heart. Noah was constantly doing his best to flirt with her and get under his brother's skin, and much to her surprise she found she liked knowing Nick was jealous. But it was Nick himself who was making her heart beat a little too quickly and her bathing suit feel uncomfortably damp, even when she was sitting in the sun.

"A penny for your thoughts," Nick said, reaching over to take Charlotte's hand. "But maybe with inflation the way it is and you being a banker I need to up my offer?"

Charlotte laughed and gave his hand a squeeze. "I was just thinking how much I like your family and how easy it is to feel the love you all have for each other. Growing up the marina was one of my favorite places in the whole world to be, and even after twelve years it still feels like home."

Nick pulled her to him and gave her a kiss that she felt all the way to her toes, and while she wasn't sure it was appropriate for a family gathering, she also wasn't sure that she cared. Looking around to see if anyone was watching, she put her arms around his neck and pulled him in close, just as Noah and the twins returned from the Jet Ski ride.

"Gross!" both girls yelled in unison.

Noah just ruffled their hair and said, "You'll understand better in a year or two."

After sharing the adventure Uncle Noah had taken them on, including how he had dumped the Jet Ski on purpose, the girls grabbed a bowl of grapes and sat down between Nick and Charlotte. Obviously, they had no intention of allowing any more gross kissing if they could help it.

"So tell me," Charlotte asked, "are you named after Pop or Uncle Nick, Miss Nikki? And whose namesake are you, Miss Steffi?"

The girls giggled at their fancy titles and shared with Charlotte the story of how they got their names.

"Mommy didn't know there was going to be two of us," Steffi said, "and she had the name Zoe picked out. When we were born, she needed two names and thought about Zoe and Zara."

"But then," Nikki said, "Mommy got really sick, and the doctor told her we would be her only babies. So, she and Daddy decided to name us after our grandparents. I'm Nicole Elizabeth after Pop and Gigi Liz, and…"

"I'm Stefanie Maria, after Papu Stefan and YaYa Maria."

Charlotte was at a loss for words, wondering what Maya had gone through the last twelve years that she didn't even know about. She remembered Maya had always wanted a house full of kids, but the two she had were beyond special.

"That's a lovely story," she said thoughtfully, "and what an honor for all your grandparents to be included in your names. I know how proud they must be."

"We don't see Gigi Liz very often," Steffi said, "but Mommy says she's really pretty, and Pop says we look like her."

Thankfully Maya and Dimitri came back from their swim before the conversation got any deeper. Charlotte knew all three of the Greyson kids had struggled with the decisions their mom had made in her lifetime, and Charlotte could certainly relate to that. Looking back, she wondered if the fact that both she and Nick had experienced hurt over their mothers' behavior was what had started their bond.

"Hey!" Maya said. "What happened to you coming out to the pier with us? I mean, it was kind of nice having some time to ourselves, but I was looking forward to catching up with you too."

Charlotte felt sheepish and turned to Nick for support, but he was enjoying watching her squirm. "Um, we did head out that way, but the waves felt good, and the next thing I knew, we were back here. I'm really sorry."

Dimitri kissed his wife's head and took pity on Charlotte. "She's just pulling your chain, Charlotte. We had a great time on the pier and in the water by ourselves, and you and Nick look very relaxed, so it appears you did as well." He gave her a wink, and Charlotte realized he thought they'd had sex instead of swimming out to meet them. *Shit, shit, shit*, this was not good!

Chapter 55

Then

After Gran's funeral there was a service at the cemetery chapel, followed by lunch at Gran's church, but by three o'clock Charlotte was back at the farm. She remembered she needed to call Becca's brother and found the number Becca had written down. She sat down in Gran's favorite rocker and held her breath as she dialed.

"Brad Huddleston's office," answered a very professional voice. "May I help you?"

"This is Charlotte Luce, and I was asked to call Mr. Huddleston today," she replied.

"One moment, Miss Luce, I have instructions to put you right through."

This couldn't be good, Charlotte thought. She'd worked long enough to know that important businesspeople didn't just sit around and wait for calls to be returned, so her thoughts were all over the place when Brad finally answered.

"Lottie," he said, his voice strong and gentle, "thank you so much for calling me today. I know your grandmother just died, and I'm so sorry for your loss, but it was imperative that we talk today."

Okay, here it comes, Charlotte thought. *I'm going to lose my cottage, or Mom did something awful. It has to be bad news.*

"I want you to come work for Olde Florida Bank," Brad told her. "The commercial banker at our Anna Maria location is retiring next month, and we need someone who knows the area and has a good head for business to step in. I just happened to be at my parents' house on Tuesday when Becca called our mom about your grandmother's passing, and I knew right away you would be perfect for this job."

Charlotte was in a state of shock. Was she really being offered a job back in Anna Maria Island? She knew nothing about banking, but she was a whiz with numbers. But was she even interested in moving back to the community of her childhood?

"I know this is a lot to take in, and I don't have to have an answer today, but I do need one by Friday. Joe Baker turned in his intent to retire on Monday, and I need to get this position filled. A month isn't very long to learn a new job. Plus, if you have to give notice where you work…"

"Yes!" exclaimed Charlotte. "I accept your offer."

Brad chuckled. "Aren't you even interested in the compensation and benefits package I have to offer you? I mean, I'm thrilled that you're interested, but I thought I would have to entice you more."

"This comes at a perfect time for me, Brad, and while I admit I should have played a little harder to get, I'm ready to come home to Florida. This sounds like the perfect opportunity."

After more discussion Brad told Charlotte to expect an official offer and HR forms in her inbox by morning. She was a little dazed when she hung up the phone, but in her heart, she knew that this was the right move for her and that Gran would have approved.

"I'm so excited for you, Lottie!" Becca cried after Charlotte shared the news with her. "And I can't wait to have you closer to us. I'm going to need lots of moral support in the next eight months, and there's nobody better than you when I need girl talk. Let's be honest—a little over a year ago I was a virgin, headed for a life in a convent, and now I'm married and going to be a mom! Who would ever have expected such a life change?"

Charlotte looked over at Jared, who was trying not to show any embarrassment at Becca's confession. He was the reason for Becca's change of heart, but Charlotte knew it had been the absolute best decision for both of them. Jared worshipped Becca, and Becca was radiant with love and pregnancy hormones. Charlotte didn't know anyone who deserved such love and happiness more than Becca.

Chapter 56

Now

Around nine o'clock Maya told the twins it was time for a bath and then bed. Despite their protests everyone could tell how worn out they were. Between the sun and the swimming, more Jet Ski rides with Uncle Noah, tons of delicious picnic food, and games of volleyball and lawn darts on the beach, it had been a long and wonderful day. To be honest, Charlotte was starting to yawn as well.

"Tell everyone good night, my sweet little guppies," Dimitri told his girls, "and Daddy will put you to bed tonight."

Nikki and Steffi made their rounds to their grandfather and both uncles, bestowing them each with a hug and a kiss. Charlotte was not expecting the same endearment to come to her, so when they wrapped their arms around her together and whispered in her ear, "We love you, Miss Lottie."

Charlotte almost broke down and cried. Hugging the pint-size beauties back, she replied, "I love you too." And she meant it.

She hated for the wonderful day to end, but she knew it was time. Looking up at Nick, she told him she needed to be going as well. She almost felt like the little girls as she hugged everyone and thanked them for the extra-special day, and then she and Nick were alone in his Jeep and headed back to her house.

"Have a good time?" Nick asked her with a sweet, heart-stopping smile.

"Better than good," Charlotte answered honestly. "It was one of the very best days of my life."

Nick brought her hand to his mouth for a kiss, but neither of them spoke again on the short ride to Charlotte's cottage. She no sooner put her key in the lock of the front door than Nick spun her around for the most passionate kiss Charlotte had ever experienced. Out of breath and not wanting to put on a show for the neighbors, she pulled him into her house.

"I've never wanted anything as much as I want you," Nick murmured in her ear, kissing and nipping down her jawline to her neck.

Charlotte was totally lost in his spell but had the strength to stop him before she made a mistake. "We need to talk about something first," she was able to tell him before her brain and body were totally under his control. Breathing heavily, Nick laid his forehead against hers and nodded.

Now that she had his attention, Charlotte didn't know how to start, but she knew for her own sanity she had to. "I don't sleep around, Nick," she told him without looking in his eyes. "I've only been with two men in my life, and I don't want to be anyone's one-night stand."

Nick was both overjoyed and scared to death. This gorgeous, smart, wonderful creature was telling him that she was practically untouched, and the man in him loved it. But the boy who still remembered how he had hurt her before worried about not hurting her again.

Taking a deep breath, Nick did his best to calm her fears. "Charlotte, I can't tell you how honored I am that you would share that with me and how much it means that you have forgiven me and are willing to trust me again. Even when we weren't together, you've been a part of every day of my life since I was ten years old, and you could never be just a one-night stand for me."

Those were the words she needed to hear, so taking his hand, she led him into her bedroom and back into her heart.

Chapter 57

Then

Three short weeks later Charlotte was back in Anna Maria Island, ready to start the next chapter of her life. Becca had enlisted the help of her mom to get Charlotte's cottage on the beach ready for her to move into, and everything had been cleaned and painted inside, waiting for Charlotte to make it her own. Mrs. Huddleston had even purchased her a comfy king-size bed, with luxurious linens, so Charlotte would at least have a nice place to sleep.

Looking around the bungalow that would now be her home, Charlotte reached for her locket and sent a kiss to heaven, once again thanking her beloved grandmother. She wasn't sure where her life would be if Gran hadn't been a part of it, but she knew her gran's blessing was one she would never forget.

The next day she walked into Olde Florida Bank as nervous as she had ever been but was quickly met with smiles and offers of help from her new assistant, Carol, and the established consumer banker, Dan. Carol was just about Charlotte's age but had started with the bank right after graduating from Pensacola Junior College, so she was the natural go-to person for Charlotte's questions. Dan was in his mid-forties, married with college-age children, and had only moved to Olde Florida from Chase Bank the year before, but he had a strong banking background. The three of them made a good team, and by the time Joe's retirement party came around, Charlotte felt comfortable in her new role.

Two years later she was an established part of the community and had brought in more new business than anyone ever had in the Anna Maria Island's location. She loved her job and had found her calling, so when Martin Riggs, CEO of Olde Florida Bank, asked her to meet him for lunch, she was scared to say the least.

Martin's office was in Orlando, where Olde Florida's home office was. Having him come to Anna Maria to meet with her was a big deal. Charlotte had recently started loving fashion, so that morning she selected her new black Armani suit with a black-and-white silk shell and black Louboutin pumps. The outfit had been her first big splurge, but she wanted to make a good impression on the man who ran a multibillion-dollar bank.

Her only jewelry was a pair of silver earrings, her watch, and, of course, the locket from Gran. As she had every morning since arriving back in Florida, she lifted up a prayer to her grandmother and once again asked for her guidance, no matter what the day would bring.

Martin had made reservations at the River House Grille in Bradenton, and Charlotte was impressed with the golf cart escorts that picked patrons up at their cars and took them to the charming restaurant on the Manatee River. She arrived shortly before the one o'clock lunch date, but Martin was already there, seated and waiting for her.

"Charlotte," he said with a smile, standing as the hostess escorted her to his table, "thank you so much for meeting with me today." He pulled out a chair for her and gave the hostess a nod, a signal of some kind, Charlotte thought, but what, and why?

"I've got to be honest with you, Charlotte," he said, getting right down to business. "When Brad Huddleston came to me and suggested you to replace Joe Baker as the commercial banker in Anna Maria, I had lots of reservations."

Oh great, here it comes, Charlotte thought. *I'm going to be fired, and the credit card bill for this outfit hasn't even come in yet!* She was lost in thought trying to figure out what had gone wrong that she missed the next words out of Martin's mouth.

"But you have exceeded the expectations of the entire board of Olde Florida Bank, which is why I came here personally to tell you that you've been named market president of the Anna Maria Island location. Congratulations, Charlotte."

At that moment the hostess came back to the table with a bottle of champagne and two crystal flutes, and it was then Charlotte realized that Martin was smiling. "Would you please repeat that?" she asked, trying not to stammer.

Martin laughed. "You've been promoted, Charlotte. You can breathe now."

The rest of the lunch was filled with Charlotte's ideas for ways to make Olde Florida even more successful in Anna Maria. Despite Martin telling her this was a celebration and she didn't have to think about work for a little while, she couldn't stop herself.

Before the lunch ended, Martin shared one more fact. "HR wouldn't approve if I told you this, but you're the first woman market president Olde Florida has ever had. And that's only because you're the first to really have the drive and the hunger that a market president needs. You'll be the youngest too. I'm telling you these things mostly so you'll know what you might be up against with the rest of the company. Sometimes we stodgy old bankers don't do well with change in the ranks." With that he gave her a friendly wink and a handshake and then added, "You'll do fine, Charlotte, and I can't tell you how pleased I am for you."

Market president, me? Charlotte thought with a smile as she drove back to Anna Maria Island. *Holy crap! I've got to call Becca!*

Chapter 58

Now

Nick backed Charlotte up against the bed, never once breaking the tsunami of a kiss that started at her bedroom door. His hands were firm against her back, stroking and touching her in ways she had never been touched before, and the blaze burning in her belly was about to consume her. The shorts and tank she had put on after swimming felt constricting and heavy, and more than anything she wanted to feel those strong hands on her bare skin.

Breaking the kiss just long enough to look into her eyes, Nick slipped his hands under her shirt and skimmed the smooth skin of her midriff with his thumbs. Charlotte was already so aroused she didn't think she could take another minute of his caresses. She closed her eyes and laid her head on his chest.

"Look at me," Nick commanded. "I want to see your face when I touch you for the first time." That about put her over the edge. Gently he pulled the tank top over Charlotte's head, smiling at her silky light-blue bra, and kneeling before her as he slipped the shorts over her long, shapely legs. Finding a matching thong, he groaned. "You remembered my favorite color," he said hoarsely, "and I like it even better now than I did when you wore that light-blue dress on my sixteenth birthday."

Charlotte was lost in a maze of erotic feelings and nostalgia. There wasn't room for both in her head right now, but Nick made it easy to stay focused. Slow kisses on her stomach had her restless for more, and before she knew it, he was on his feet, slipping the straps of her bra almost leisurely over her shoulders before reaching around to unclasp it. When her full breasts finally fell free, Nick stared at her in amazement. "Fucking gorgeous," he growled before taking them in his hands.

When he ran his tongue over her swollen and throbbing nipples, Charlotte cried out. "Please, Nick, please. I need…"

"You need what, Charlotte?" he asked. "Tell me what you need."

I need you inside of me, she thought. *I need an orgasm, and I need for you to be in love with me. Shit, shit, shit, where did that come from?*

But Charlotte wouldn't answer, although she moaned a lot, so Nick continued his tortuous assault on her body. Finally, he slipped his fingers into the thin elastic band of her thong and slowly pulled it down to her knees. He looked at the patch of soft red curls between her legs and right back up into her eyes, and Charlotte panicked. *Should I have gotten waxed?* she wondered. She had thought before about a trip to the spa, but somehow it hadn't felt right to her. Now she was having second thoughts. Nick was probably used to women who were always bare below, and the thought was making her self-conscious and maybe even a little jealous.

"You're so natural, Charlotte," Nick said, his voice deep with desire. "I can't tell you what a turn-on it is for me."

He started kissing her stomach again, the kisses traveling lower and lower, and then he gently laid her down on the bed. Teasing and caressing her delicate flesh with his fingers, he moved his head down between her thighs, and Charlotte came right up off of the bed. Early in her relationship with Ryan, he had tried to go down on her, but Charlotte wasn't having any part of it. Whether it was from her body image issues or just the unknown, she wasn't sure, but eventually Ryan had quit trying, and Peter had never asked, so it had never occurred to her that Nick would.

"Stop." She squirmed. "You don't have to do that." But Nick just kept going, and damn if it didn't feel good. Actually, it felt amazing, but that didn't stop her from trying once more to get him to stop.

168

"Charlotte," Nick said, looking directly into her eyes, "relax," and she did.

Never in the history of orgasms was there one as strong and as deep as the one that welled up in Charlotte. She cried out as it racked through her body, but Nick didn't stop his attention until she was totally still.

When it was over, he climbed up on the bed and kissed her. Charlotte was almost afraid of how the kiss would taste but was surprised. *Nothing at all like I imagined,* she thought, wrapping her arms around his neck. Nick pressed against her and holy crap! She had forgotten about that monster between his legs, and from the feel of it on her belly, the monster was ready to play.

Breaking the kiss, she thought of a nice way to tell him there was no way in hell that thing would fit inside of her. Nick must have read her thoughts, because he chuckled and said, "It will be okay, Charlotte; I promise. I'll go slow until you're comfortable."

Comfortable! A sledgehammer between my legs would probably be more comfortable, she thought, but she knew there was no turning back now.

Somewhere between her awesome orgasm and her attempts to figure out how to accommodate Nick's girth, he had stripped out of his clothes and laid a six-pack of condoms on her nightstand. *Six!* Was he trying to kill her?

But as quickly as the doubts had started, desire once again overtook her as Nick started nibbling on her neck and giving lots of attention to her throbbing breasts. When he spread her legs and slipped between them, she wanted nothing more than to have him put out the inferno building again inside, even if it meant doing a little snake charming.

"Are you okay?" he asked her, taking his time

Charlotte nodded. She was definitely aware that she was being stretched wide open, but she wanted the ache between her legs to be satisfied, and with every inch and every thrust, she felt closer and closer to having the fire put out.

Nick was a master at knowing just where to touch and just where to kiss, but it was when he took her head in his hands and once again said, "Look at me," that she lost it. Wave after wave of feelings, pure and raw, washed over her and she cried out from the most delicious sensations she had ever experienced.

Nick was right behind her, calling out her name as if it were a prayer, and then for a few moments they just lay there. After all these years they were both thinking the same thing. Was it as incredible as they had hoped it would be? And the answer for both was hell yes!

Chapter 59

Now

Nick brushed a long strawberry-blonde lock from Charlotte's face and gave her another long, slow kiss as he gently broke apart from her. Charlotte winced at the movement. Seeing the look on her face, he brushed his hand over her face and asked, "Are you sure you're okay?"

Okay? She was more than okay, she wanted to say. She was worn out and sore, but she had never felt better in her life. But instead she smiled and closed her eyes while Nick disposed of the evidence and headed naked into her kitchen. A naked man in her kitchen? Now that was a first for Charlotte Luce!

When Nick returned, he was carrying a large glass of ice water, and he offered it to her as he sat down on the bed. "I was hoping for wine," Charlotte said with a pout.

"But you need to rehydrate," Nick responded with a laugh. "Wine is for before; water is for after."

Charlotte accepted the glass and drank it all down, surprised at how thirsty she was. "Is this one of those G-man things you told me about, Special Agent?"

"Just experience," he responded, and then seeing the hurt in her eyes, he realized that had been the wrong thing to say. "I meant experience from working out, Charlotte, because we just had a workout equal to a five-mile run."

Relief washed over her face, and he asked, "May I stay?"

Charlotte nodded and pulled the sheet back, giving Nick an up-close view of her curvaceous body. He smiled with appreciation of the beautiful woman she had become and climbed into bed and embraced her, stroking her hair and kissing her head like she was treasured and adored.

It had been so long since a man had held her after sex, and before she knew it, Charlotte was running her fingers over his glorious chest and abs, and yep, round two was about to begin!

It was early on Sunday morning and Charlotte was having a wonderful dream. She and Nick were playing on the beach, and he was burying her in the sand. The warmth of the sun was beating down, and both of their faces were locked in smiles like they had a secret the world didn't know about. Then all of a sudden, the bell from an ice cream truck was right behind them. She knew the ice cream truck wasn't allowed on the beach, but the ringing wouldn't stop. As much as she liked ice cream, she really just wanted to go back to the peacefulness of the moment.

The ringing broke through her consciousness, and Charlotte opened her eyes with a start. She was curled in Nick's arms, her back to his front, and one of his powerful legs was draped over hers, holding her in place. "Nick," she moaned, trying to wake up and move from under his massive body, "your phone is ringing."

Without even turning over, he grabbed his cell from the nightstand and spoke into it. "Greyson," he answered out of habit.

"Well, good morning, Uncle Nick," his brother, Noah, teased. "The ladies have been wondering where you are, so I told them about your early-morning run and how you were then picking up Charlotte for brunch. Dimi is cooking this morning. We're eating in just about an hour, but that's plenty of time for, you know, a little more running." Noah was still laughing when he hung up the phone, but Nick wasn't nearly as amused.

He muttered under his breath and turned to the sleepy redhead lying beside him. "This is not how I wanted this morning to go," he said apologetically, "but I forgot that Maya and her family stayed at the marina last night, and the twins aren't quite old enough to understand grown-up sleepovers." Pulling her even closer, he started massaging her shoulders, her back, and on down to her very womanly backside before slipping his hand between her legs. Nipping at her ear, he took her moans of pleasure as a green light, so he reached past his phone on the nightstand for a condom, finding only two left. Wow! What a night it had been!

Charlotte tried to beg out of going to brunch with him, but Nick wasn't having any part of it. "I don't need to be there, Nick," she said. "This is your family, and I was with them all day yesterday."

"Oh no, Miss Charlotte," he laughed. "Everyone is expecting you, and Nikki and Steffi will be very disappointed if you're not there."

"But," she almost whispered, "everyone will know you were here all night, and it all feels kind of like a walk of shame."

Nick's eyes turned dark. "Are you ashamed of what we did, Charlotte?" he asked softly.

"Oh, no! No, Nick, it's not that at all. I just don't want to be the brunt of anyone's jokes." She put her arms around his neck and pulled him close. "I guess inside I'm still that self-conscious teenage girl you knew a lifetime ago, and I'm not sure that I'm strong enough to be anything else."

"That teenage girl was my best friend, but I'm pretty fond of the woman she's become. You are stronger than you give yourself credit for, Charlotte, and I promise you no one will give you a hard time or make you feel uncomfortable. Noah is going to be unmerciful to me with his crap, but he'll find a way to do it when no one else is around." He gave her the look that had always turned her tummy inside out; what could she do but agree to go with him?

"How about you jump in the shower," Nick said with a devilish grin on his face, "and I'll go pop one of those fancy pods into your coffee machine and bring you a cup? I've got a clean shirt in the Jeep, so I'll join you as soon as I get it."

Charlotte groaned. It may have been the best sex of her life, but the minute she got out of bed, she realized how sore she was. She was definitely not up for another rodeo, so she gave him a halfhearted smile and tried to redirect his attention. "Or maybe," she said, "I can shower while you make the coffee and get your shirt, and then you can shower while I get dressed. Wouldn't that be more efficient?"

Watching her walk into the bathroom, Nick couldn't help but laugh. "I'm not sure about the efficiency," he chuckled, "but I can see that you might want some time alone, so go ahead and shower, and your coffee will be waiting on you when you get out."

Even the thought of putting on shorts made her wince, so Charlotte decided on a lightweight, flouncy skirt and a pair of old-fashioned white cotton panties. The edges were trimmed with lace, so at least they were pretty, but there was no way anything lacy, silky, or sexy was going to touch her swollen flesh! A hot shower and dusting of cornstarch baby powder helped some, but she knew sitting through brunch with Nick's family was going to be an effort.

When they arrived at the marina, Nick stopped her before she could get out of the Jeep. "Are you sure you're okay?" he asked seriously, searching her bright green eyes for the truth.

"Well," she answered truthfully, "I feel as if I've been thoroughly fucked, but it was worth every minute of it."

"When did you start talking like that, Charlotte Luce?" Nick grinned. "I'm both shocked and oddly aroused at the same time."

He took her hand and led her toward the deck, never letting go, even when his family turned to welcome them. Charlotte never felt more at ease than at that moment. She squeezed his hand and kept hers firmly in place.

Brunch was about to be served, and Nick was right—no one said a word about him being out all night or the fact that he had been with Charlotte. Dimitri had fixed a smorgasbord of traditional Greek breakfast foods, and the homemade pastries were definitely calling Charlotte's name, and she was thrilled to see a large platter of sliced fruit and a bowl of yogurt nestled between the goodies.

Helping herself to a dish of yogurt covered with fruit, she sat down gingerly and enjoyed the family's morning conversation. Trying to get comfortable on her chair, she looked up to see Noah watching her, and he winked. Noah winked at her a lot, and she tried to tell herself he was being his normal flirtatious self, but that didn't stop the blush spreading from her head to her toes.

"It's been so great spending time with you, Charlotte," Maya said as she was packing up her family after everything was cleaned up. "Holidays are the only times we close the restaurant. Promise me you'll come back to Tarpon Springs so we can really get to know each other, okay? I would love to be able to stay here longer, but we promised Dimi's family we would be with them this afternoon and tomorrow, and the girls are looking forward to seeing all their Maras cousins."

Charlotte didn't realize Pop had walked up behind her until he said, "Maybe someday they'll have some Greyson cousins too. I'm not getting any younger, you know, and I'd love to have more grandkids to spoil."

Charlotte looked up to see both Nick and Noah looking her way. She took the coward's way out of the discussion and changed the subject. Reaching down, she gave Maya a hug and said, "Of course I'll come to see you, and when I do, I'll want a big box of Dimi's famous chocolate baklava to bring back to my team at the bank. It was delicious.

Nikki and Steffi said their good-byes to their grandfather and uncles and then turned to Charlotte. "When you come to see Mommy, will you visit with us too?" Nikki asked.

"We have a playhouse and lots of dolls, and we promise we'll share them with you," Steffi added.

Charlotte bent down and took the two girls in her arms. "I most definitely will come to see you, and I look forward to meeting your dollies," she told them. The girls hugged her in return and skipped out to the van for the ride back to Tarpon.

When the Maras family was on their way, Pop announced he was going to sit on the deck with a good book because even though Monday was a holiday, he planned to open the marina. Noah had a hot date with a new woman he had met at a fishing tournament, so he said good-bye and headed to the door.

"I look forward to catching up with you, big brother," he said to Nick with a huge grin on his face. "You and Lottie enjoy the rest of the weekend, and we'll talk soon."

Nick flashed him the bird, which only made Noah laugh, and then he was gone.

Chapter 60

Now

"That just leaves us," Nick said softly to Charlotte, "and I know just what we need to do."

Shit, shit, shit! she thought. *I can barely sit down, and he's ready for an encore? Where in the world did his stamina come from?* But she said nothing and smiled sweetly as he led her to his Jeep and headed back toward her bungalow.

Once they were safely inside, Nick took her in his arms and kissed her. "Take that cute little skirt off and get into bed," he told her. "I'll be there in a minute."

"Uh, Nick," she started, but he put his finger to her lips and silenced her.

"Into bed, woman," he commanded. Turning her toward her bedroom, he gave her a swat on the bottom, chuckling at the look on her face.

Once her skirt was off, Charlotte pulled down the sheets and climbed into her big, comfy bed. Burrowing her head into the pillows, she breathed in a whiff of strong, sexy male, and her face got hot as she remembered what all had happened there last night. She was running the reel of the night's activities through her head when Nick came into the room carrying a cold beer.

"Is that for me?" she asked. "Or are we sharing?" When they were kids, they had thought nothing of sharing each other's drinks, but it had been a long time since she had thought about sharing a can of anything with someone else.

"It's all for you," Nick replied, "but it's not to drink." He moved to the side of her bed and sat down. "Spread your legs for me."

Charlotte shook her head and glared. *What kind of kink is he into?* she screamed inside. *I've read a lot of books with sex scenes, and beer was never a part of them.*

Nick ran his free hand through his hair and sighed. "Do you ever just do what you're asked, Charlotte? I'm trying to help you here; can you please just trust me?"

That's easy for him to say, she inwardly sulked. *I feel as if I'm sitting on a burning bush, and he wants to play games?* She was all ready to tell him what he could do with his beer when he started to talk.

"When Maya was pregnant with the girls, she had a lot of swelling and pain, you know, down there," he said, swirling his hand in the direction of said swelling. "One day I stopped in unexpectedly to see her and found her propped up in bed with a cold can of beer between her legs. Needless to say, we were both a little horrified, but Dimi told me later that it really helped her. Anyway, I thought maybe it would help you too."

Nick held the beer out for her to take, and Charlotte smiled. He really was thinking of her, and that made her heart and her tummy do wild, crazy things. She slowly spread her legs and rested the icy-cold beer right where it hurt. "It's so cold," she cried out, "but it feels so good."

Nick climbed into the bed and kissed her softly on the lips. "The rest of my plan is for us to take a nap," he said, pulling her close. "And by nap, I mean sleep. I don't think either one of us got much last night."

Charlotte snuggled down into the mattress, safe in Nick's arms, with a cold can of beer between her thighs. She was still smiling when she drifted off to sleep.

Chapter 61

Now

When Charlotte finally opened her eyes and looked at the clock beside the bed, she was surprised to see how late it was. She couldn't remember the last time she had taken a nap in the middle of the day, but stretching her long limbs, she realized how refreshed she felt. She reached over to the other side of the bed and was disappointed to find it empty.

"Nick?" she called out, not sure if he was even still there.

He opened the bedroom door and greeted her. "Hey there, sleepyhead. I guess you really needed that nap." He smiled, in that heart-stopping way he had. "I just ordered pizza. I hope you're hungry."

Damn, he was hot standing there in his Skivvies! But she was hungry, the meager breakfast of yogurt and fruit long since forgotten. Her stomach was rumbling, and pizza sounded delicious, especially with an icy-cold beer. Beer! The image of a beer can settled between her legs turned her beet red from head to toe, and her first thought was, *where did it go?*

"Looking for this?" Nick grinned, pulling the can from behind his back. "It had lost its therapeutic effect by the time I got up, so I moved it. Nice panties by the way."

Pulling the covers over her head, Charlotte yelled, "Go away!"

Instead Nick sat down on the bed. "Come on," he said. "Don't be that way. I loved your lacy thong, and your schoolgirl panties are quite a turn-on too, but they're just window dressing. Even in a pair of boxer shorts you'd look sexy. Come pick out a movie to watch so we can cuddle on the couch and eat pizza, like we used to."

"I don't believe we ever watched movies in our underwear," she retorted, "but there's a first for everything!" As she swung her legs over the side of the bed, she realized the soreness between them had started to subside. She might be able to walk normally someday after all. Thank heaven for that!

A couple of hours later, full on pizza and very relaxed on beer, Charlotte turned to Nick with tears in her eyes. "I could watch *Titanic* every day and never get tired of it," she sighed. "It's the best love story ever."

Charlotte loved the way that Nick was stroking her hair and smiling. She remembered all the times they had watched *Titanic* together, and even though the ending was the same, she always cried and always deemed it the best love story ever. She didn't know any other guy who would willingly watch a chick flick more than once, but he had never told her no.I need to ask you a question," she said as Nick wiped the tears from her cheeks.

"Okay, what's your question?"

"Why didn't you try to come after me when I took off for Indiana?"

Nick exhaled and rubbed his hand over his jaw. "You want to talk about this *now*?" he asked.

"Well, I think Jack would have gone after Rose, so after everything you told me about back then, I was just wondering why you didn't try to come after me."

"I did try, Charlotte," he told her, lightly kissing her hair. "More than anything I wanted to talk with you, but you blocked my calls and had Becca tell me you were with her mom, remember? When I found out you had gone to Indiana, I knew I needed to go there so we could talk face-to-face, and that meant telling my dad what had happened."

Charlotte sat up and looked into Nick's beautiful blue eyes, waiting for him to continue.

"In my entire life the only time Pop has ever told me he was disappointed in me was the night of the senior send-off, when I confessed to him everything that had happened. He wasn't happy that I had been drinking or that I'd let Ashley compromise my integrity, as he put it, but mostly he was angry I had hurt you. But he said he would support me going to Indiana. He even said I could take his truck, but first I had to get your mom's blessing."

"You talked to my mom, Nick? Why is it I'm just now hearing about this?"

The emotion in Charlotte's voice was strong, so he chose his next words carefully. "Because she told me if I really cared about you, I would let you have a chance to find your own way at IU, without the baggage of an out-of-state relationship. I hated it, but I understood what she was saying, so I let you go."

"She had no right to do that!" Charlotte cried, trying to hold back the old feelings that were threatening to boil over. "She knew how miserable I was, yet she kept me from the one thing that would have made things better.

"Don't blame your mom, Charlotte. She had just come from taking you to the airport, and her heart was feeling the loss too. She read me the riot act; that's for sure. For the first time I saw Maggie Luce act like a real mom, and I have to tell you, it had an impact on me. I thought between your mom and your gran you would be okay and that I would just be a reminder of what might have been."

Charlotte took his face in her hands and looked up at the man she had loved for almost all her life. "I loved my gran so much, and I love my mom too, but I was never okay after what happened, despite having two strong women in my life. I got past it, and in some respects, I grew from it, but my mom should have at least told me you wanted to come after me. I'm sorry that all these years I thought you didn't even care enough to say good-bye."

"Saying good-bye was the last thing in the world I wanted to do," he told her gently. Then, taking her lips in his, he gave her a kiss that was anything but gentle.

Chapter 62

Now

The Fourth of July was a big day on Anna Maria Island, and Nick and Charlotte didn't want to miss a minute of it. As much as she loved to eat, Charlotte had never been much of a cook, but she did manage to whip Nick up some scrambled eggs and toast, so they wouldn't have to waste time at a restaurant. After the pizza splurge the night before, Charlotte settled on a fresh Georgia peach and two cups of black coffee.

"Is that your normal breakfast?" Nick asked. "I don't think you eat enough."

Oh no, not this from another man! she thought. First Peter had tried to get her to eat less, and now Nick wanted her to eat more. Why couldn't they just support her? After all, she was healthy, and wasn't that the main thing?

"How about we enjoy the day and leave my eating habits out of it?" she said as politely as possible. "I won't warn you of the dangers of eating too much cholesterol, and you won't warn me of the dangers of too much fruit. Deal?"

Nick grabbed her around the waist and pulled her down onto his lap. "Deal," he agreed with a grin. Without letting her go, he finished his breakfast.

The Privateers' pirate parade started at ten a.m. and was always a big hit with the community. The route went from Coquina Beach to the

City Pier. Nick and Charlotte had always watched from the roof of the marina when they were kids, and he wanted that same view today.

"Really, Nick? You want to climb on top of the roof like we did in high school? I hate to break it to you, old man, but we aren't kids anymore."

Nick hadn't been home on the Fourth of July for years, and he was not about to be deterred. He wanted the same experience they'd had on the last Independence Day they had shared so Charlotte reluctantly agreed. At the marina, Nick couldn't find his dad anywhere, but when he went to the shed to get the ladder, he found it already propped up against the building.

"Who's up there?" Nick yelled.

Both his dad and his brother called back down to him.

"We thought you'd never get here," Noah laughed. "Grab your pretty lady and get your asses up here before you miss the beginning of the parade! I hear there's going to be some lovely wenches on the pirate boat this year, and I don't want to miss them!"

As always, the parade brought smiles and fond memories for Charlotte. Sitting on the roof of the marina with three of her favorite men, she felt more at peace than she had in a long time. Without even thinking about it, she reached up and touched her locket and gave a mental kiss to her gran.

"Since Pop is officially working today, why don't Nick and I go get some chicken, and we'll all have a picnic on the deck," Noah offered. "We need some bro time anyway, right, big brother?"

Nick groaned at the prospect of being alone with Noah, knowing that he was going to want some insider information about his last two days with Charlotte, but she and his dad thought it was a wonderful plan, so what could he do but agree?

Chapter 63

Now

Only a few customers came by the marina, allowing Pop to spend most of the day with his family. After their picnic, Nick took Charlotte on a Jet Ski ride, and they swam in the gulf with Noah. All too soon it was time for the fireworks on the beach.

With blankets and a cooler of beer in his hands, Nick led Charlotte out onto the sand and set up a cozy spot for them to watch the colorful pyrotechnic show in the sky. Pulling her between his legs, he nibbled gently on her ear and turned her face toward his. "This weekend has been amazing," he said huskily. "Never in my wildest dreams could I have made it any better."

Charlotte touched his cheek and smiled. "It has been special, Nick," she said, "but weekends have to end."

Nick cleared his throat and sighed. "Well, here's the thing. My vacation time has ended too, and I have to start back to work tomorrow. My plan is to leave for Tampa about four a.m. so I can beat the traffic."

Charlotte was quiet for a moment, trying to come up with the right thing to say. "I understand, Nick," she said finally. "Your life is in Tampa, but I'm grateful we had the time to sort out our past."

"The past doesn't have to define our future, Charlotte," Nick said firmly. "I told you I wasn't looking for a one-night stand, or even a weekend fling, so I will be back. In fact, let's make a date right now for Friday evening to go to MarVista and eat out on the beach."

Charlotte thought her heart was going to burst. He was coming back, and maybe, just maybe they could find a way to make this last. "It's a date" was all she said.

When the fireworks were over, and everything had been cleaned up and put away, Nick gave his dad a hug and told him he would see him over the weekend. Noah had met one of the "wenches" from the parade and had left earlier, but Pop was grinning seeing Nick and Charlotte together again.

"You don't have to have an excuse to come back, Lottie," Pop told her. "My home and my heart are always open for you."

Trying to hold back the tears, Charlotte wrapped her arms around the gentle giant and gave his cheek a kiss. "I know that now," she said with a smile. She gave Pop's hand a final squeeze, and she and Nick headed for her cottage.

The minute they were inside the door, Nick took her in his arms and kissed her like there was no tomorrow. They were hungry for each other, but Nick took his time worshipping every inch of her body. When they were both sated but still wrapped together, Charlotte realized this had been more than sex; they had made love.

Chapter 64

Now

How am I going to get that in my mouth? Charlotte wondered. She was sitting cross-legged on her bed looking at the glory of Nick's naked sleeping form, wanting to give him something to remember her by. It was three in the morning, and she had lain awake all night thinking about everything that had happened since he'd come back to town. Then it had hit her that she really wanted to give him what Ashley hadn't that night twelve years ago.

The problem was, even without saluting her, the sleeping beast looked enormous, and after her debacle at IU, she needed to make sure she did this right! Carefully she moved down on the bed, and gathering all her courage, she ran her tongue down the length of him. *Not a bad start,* she congratulated herself.

With a little more bravado, she gently licked the tip and then carefully took it into her mouth. Who knew just that little bit of contact would wake a sleeping FBI agent?

"What the...?" Nick asked, almost falling out of bed. When he looked down and saw a mass of strawberry-blonde curls hovering over his lower body and felt the warmth of her velvet mouth, the monster roared to life, and Charlotte's eyes almost popped out of her head. "What are you doing?" he asked, even though he knew *what* she was doing.

Wrapping her hand around him, at least as far as it would go, she looked up and smiled at him. "Relax," she told him, just as he had told her on Saturday night. "Think of this as a parting gift," Charlotte said, and then she wrapped her lips around him and went back to work.

Just as she was getting into a nice rhythm, if she did say so herself, Nick reached down and lifted her up and right onto his now throbbing and very awake erection. "I'll show you a parting gift," he said, taking control of the situation, and what a parting gift it was!

Charlotte laid her head on Nick's chest as she tried to catch her breath. Even through the soreness and the burn, it had been over the top. She lay still a while longer, knowing once she moved off of him he would need to get in the shower and head for home. Of course, looking him in the eye after her attempted oral adventure was going to be difficult too.

Finally, Nick lifted her head, and the look on his face was one she would always remember. "You are one amazing surprise after another, and I wish I could find the words to describe how I feel right now." Running his hands down her back, he closed his eyes for a minute and said, "I have never experienced anything as erotic and wonderful as what we just did, but, Charlotte, we didn't use a condom."

Shit, shit, shit! Leave it to her to forget about something that important. Both Ryan and Peter had always used a condom, so she wasn't concerned about having any nasty diseases, but what did she really know about Nick's sex life? For all she knew he could be a man whore!

"I just had a physical before I came home," Nick went on, "and I'm clean. Plus, it's been a while for me, so… Anyway, I don't want you to worry, okay?" He looked at her with such hope and such concern that she couldn't help but melt.

"I'm not worried." She smiled and thought, *It's Noah who's the man whore anyway, not Nick.*

After a quick shower and a cup of coffee for the road, it was time for Nick to leave. "I hate to go, but you'd probably get tired of me if I was underfoot all the time," he tried to joke. As tears started to form in her eyes, he gave her one last kiss and said, "Charlotte, I—"

"Go," she told him with a grin. "You're not the only one who has to go back to work today!" But inside, her heart was begging him to stay.

He gave her one more heart-stopping smile and said, "I'll see you on Friday," and then he was out the door.

Chapter 65

Now

The day after a holiday was always especially busy at the bank, and this one was no different. Customers were waiting in the foyer by eight thirty, so at eight forty-five Charlotte rallied her team and told them they needed to open a few minutes early. Normally the customer service representative, Pam, took care of new accounts and pretty much anything other than processing transactions, but she was on vacation, which meant Carol had to step into that role, leaving Charlotte on her own.

It was eleven thirty before Charlotte had a moment to breathe and check her e-mails, and there was one from Nick. "I made it home safely but miss you already. Nick."

Charlotte's heart swelled, but she was cautious in her reply, not wanting to sound like one of *those girls*. "Glad you made it home okay. Have a great day!" There, that didn't sound needy at all, right?

By the time she was able to leave the bank at six thirty, Charlotte was exhausted, but she knew she owed her mom a call. She had promised to call her back on Saturday to hear all about Thomas and their upcoming marriage, but everything had changed when Nick invited her to the marina for his family's party on Saturday.

After throwing on a pair of shorts and a T-shirt, she grabbed a yogurt and an apple to eat while she and her mom talked. What she really wanted to do was call Becca, but she had to put priorities first. She unlocked her cell, but before she could place the call, she noticed she had a message. "I made reservations for Friday night at 7:30. Pick you up at 6:00. N." The message was followed by a winking smiley face emoji.

What are we, Nick, sixteen? Charlotte laughed to herself, but truth be told, she loved it! She texted back a simple "See you then" and called her mom.

"Hey, Mom," she said when Maggie answered. "Sorry I didn't get you called back on Saturday, but something came up." Oh yeah, something *big* had come up, but of course she wasn't going to tell her mom that!

"I assume it had something to do with Nick Greyson, am I right?"

Charlotte could hear the disapproving tone in her mom's voice, but she wasn't going to discuss Nick with her. She was hurt and a little angry that her mom had never told her about Nick's visit the day she'd left for Indiana, but she couldn't change what had happened, and this call was about her mom. "I want to talk about you and Thomas, Mom. Tell me all about this man who's captured your heart and all about your wedding plans."

For the next thirty minutes Maggie shared her love story with her daughter, and Charlotte did her best to listen and stay involved. Truthfully, she was having a hard time keeping her eyes open after a night without sleep and a busy day at work, so when Maggie said she would talk with her soon, Charlotte was only too happy to end the call.

She was just about to put her phone on to charge and get ready for bed when she saw she had another message. "You're killing me here," it read. "Sweet dreams, beautiful."

Felling pretty proud of herself for keeping her feelings in check, she turned off her phone and got into bed without even brushing her teeth. She needed sleep, and she was ready for those sweet dreams.

With Pam on vacation, Wednesday was still a busy day at the bank, but Charlotte found some time to go out on client calls. The Lisa Marie Fernandez multicolor linen shirtdress she had chosen that morning was perfect for the sultry Florida weather, and the low-heeled, strappy tan sandals were just right for walking around the construction site of the new drugstore she had secured the financing for. She was feeling really good about the new business she was bringing in for Olde Florida, so when she started to pass the marina, she decided to stop in.

"Lottie!" Pop said with joy. "What brings you here today?"

"I was just driving by and thought I would say hello and thank you again for your hospitality this weekend. I enjoyed every minute of it."

Pop pulled her into a big hug, and Charlotte felt the love that she'd been missing for so many years. "I meant what I said, Lottie; you're always welcome here. Can you stay for a glass of lemonade? I just made some fresh."

"I've got to get back to work, but I appreciate the offer. I'll see you soon, though," she said, hoping that would be over the upcoming weekend.

The rest of the afternoon was crazy busy, and once again it was six thirty before Charlotte left work. She picked up a spinach salad with avocado and shrimp for dinner, and once she was settled in, she dialed Becca. She'd received an e-mail earlier from Nick saying his day sucked, and he was thinking about her, but no texts or cute emoji's. She didn't really know much about his job, but she understood that he was just as busy as she was. By the time Becca answered, Charlotte was ready to tell her best friend all about the developments with Nick, including the spectacular orgasms. Yeah, especially those!

Chapter 66

Now

By noon on Thursday, Charlotte still hadn't heard anything else from Nick, and even though she was disappointed, she didn't let herself dwell on it. After all, they were adults, and there was no commitment between them, just a weekend of mind-blowing sex. Still, after his messages on Tuesday, it hurt a little. She had plenty of work to do if she wanted to get out on time Friday, though. She put Nick out of her thoughts and focused on banking.

As soon as she got home on Thursday evening, Charlotte threw a load of towels in the washer and changed into her running clothes. She hoped to be wrapped in the arms of a sexy FBI agent on Saturday morning, so she wanted to get a run in now.

The beach was her favorite place to run in the evening, and tonight she kept thinking back to lying on the beach with Nick, snuggled between his legs as they watched the fireworks. She knew she was smiling as she passed Mrs. Danvers's cottage, and she mentally promised herself to visit with her friend one evening the next week. She hadn't even told Mrs. D about the breakup with Peter, and now she had the budding relationship with Nick to share.

After an extra-long run, Charlotte returned home ready for some food and a big glass of Beach House white. She checked her phone as she poured the wine, but there were no texts or e-mails from Nick.

Taking a huge gulp of wine to steady her nerves, she did her best to not read anything into his silence, but it got harder by the minute.

Before sitting down to eat, she put the towels in the dryer and her sheets in the washer. After all, she wanted her bed to be fresh and comfy for the next night. *But what if he doesn't show?* she thought. *Surely I didn't read things so wrong that he's changed his mind in less than forty-eight hours.*

As good as her dinner had sounded, Charlotte just picked at it, no longer hungry, but she did help herself to a refill of wine. By ten her laundry was done, clean sheets were on the bed, and she was a little buzzed. Deciding she needed a good night's sleep, she took a quick shower to remove the side effects of her run, put on her IU T-shirt, and climbed into bed.

Where are you, Nick? was her last thought as she drifted into a wine-induced slumber.

Chapter 67

Now

Charlotte was deep in sleep, the sky still dark outside of her bedroom window, when the landline on her bedside table started to ring. Looking at the clock, she saw it was just after four and grew worried. Calls at this time of day were never good.

Taking a deep breath for courage, she answered on the third ring. "Hello," she said tentatively, hoping it was a wrong number. She was surprised to hear the voice of Martin Riggs, CEO of Olde Florida Bank.

"Charlotte," he began, "I'm sorry to have to wake you so early, but we have a situation, and I'm going to need you to meet me at your office at six thirty." Sighing in a way Charlotte had never heard from him before, he continued, "Carol Neel and her brother, Tony, were arrested last night, and we need to be ready for damage control before the staff and our clients find out about it."

Charlotte was at a loss for words. The half bottle of wine from the night before had to be keeping her brain from waking up, because surely he hadn't just said Carol had been arrested. "I'm lost, Martin," she told him. "Why would Carol and Tony be arrested together, and what does that have to do with the bank?"

"They've been charged with money laundering, check kiting, and racketeering, and right now the FBI is invoking the RICO Act. In my thirty-plus years of banking, I've never seen anything like it."

Charlotte gasped and put her hand on her chest in hopes of steadying her racing heart. "Did you say FBI, Martin?" she asked trembling.

"Evidently they've been working on this for months and investigating on the island for the last few weeks. I talked with the regional director, and he promised not to let the word out until a nine a.m. press conference, which is why we need to get on top of this now."

Charlotte wasn't sure she could even speak. Investigating on the island for the last few weeks? It didn't take a rocket scientist to figure out who had been doing the investigating, but she crossed her fingers and asked anyway. "Did the director happen to give you the name of the agent doing the investigation? Anna Maria Island isn't that big. I would think a stranger coming to town asking questions would draw some attention."

"A guy by the name of Nick Greyson," Martin told her. "He evidently was raised on the island, and his family still lives there, so it didn't raise any red flags having him hang around. Listen, Charlotte, I'm on the road, and I need to make some other calls, so I'll see you around six thirty at your office."

Charlotte stared at the phone in disbelief and then ran to the bathroom to throw up. There really wasn't any food in her stomach, but once she had expelled the acid, the dry heaves continued. With tears streaming down her face and her head hanging over the toilet, she really just wanted to die.

"How could you have done this, Nick?" she sobbed. Finding the strength to get up from the bathroom floor, she stumbled to her bed and let out all the sorrow she was feeling. Her pillow, the one Nick had slept on just a few days ago, was soon soaked with her tears, and her bed, where she had felt the most intense connection of her life, now felt like a coffin—her coffin and the place she knew her heart was finally going to be laid to rest.

Chapter 68

Now

Finally, all cried out, Charlotte got up and into the hottest shower she could stand. She felt dirty, and her skin was crawling. Even her favorite body wash couldn't remove the feeling of betrayal and despair that had settled deep inside. There wasn't time to wash her hair, so she pulled it into a ponytail and then took a good look at herself in the mirror.

Just a few days ago her cheeks had held the glow of serious lovemaking, but now they were pale and hollow looking. Her lips, which had been swollen and pink from hours of intense kissing, were now drawn and thin. She knew she couldn't face Martin and her team looking like a zombie, so she searched around in her makeup drawer for something stronger than blush. Coming up with some tinted moisturizer, she covered her face and then added concealer, mascara, and eye shadow and finished up with lots of blush. It wasn't the natural look she preferred, but it was better than going to work looking like Ghost Girl.

Taking a swig of Pepto-Bismol right out of the bottle and grabbing a sleeve of saltines to help her queasy stomach, Charlotte headed to the bank. Thankfully it was dress-down day, because she wasn't sure she could have stood getting into a suit to meet with Martin. Knowing that they were both going to need lots of coffee, she hadn't even turned her Keurig on, opting instead to make a strong pot at work.

The sun was just coming up as she pulled into the parking lot, and the last thing she wanted to do was go inside. As she reached up for her locket, she could feel more tears starting to build, but she knew she couldn't let them fall. Taking every bit of courage she had, she closed her eyes and talked with her gran. "I know you said that wherever I went you'd be with me, Gran, but right now I feel like I'm in hell, and that's no place for you. So if you can please just help me through this, I promise I'll try to be the granddaughter you deserved from now on."

After punching in her code to turn off the alarms, Charlotte stepped into the break room to start the coffee. As she headed to her office, two things happened at once: Martin knocked on the door, and she looked over and saw Carol's desk. She was hurt and angry and in a state of denial, but one thing she knew for sure was that Carol would never have gotten involved in something illegal. Right then Charlotte knew she would do everything in her power to clear her assistant's name.

"Good morning, Charlotte," Martin said as he entered the bank. She could see the stress and the concern on his face, and it pleased her to know he had come all this way to talk with the staff himself. She knew someone with less prominence within the bank could have handled it, but having Martin there gave her some of the courage she needed.

They each poured themselves a large mug of coffee and headed to Charlotte's office to debrief. Charlotte had so many questions, but out of respect for his position, she allowed Martin to go first.

"Apparently Tony Neel has had quite a gambling problem for the last decade. As long as he was winning, everything was okay, but about three years ago he came into a really bad streak and borrowed money from a loan shark in Cuba. You can imagine how that went. He kept losing and kept borrowing until he was in so deep that he had no choice but to play or pay."

Martin stopped for a minute and took a drink of coffee, and Charlotte took advantage of the opening. "But how does this affect, Carol?" she asked cautiously. "She lives simply, shops at discount stores, and the car she drives is five years old. Is it just guilt by association?"

Martin shook his head. "The FDIC has been performing an audit of Olde Florida, this location especially, and they have evidence that Carol has been helping her brother. It's not as strong a case against her as it is with Tony, but the FBI may be using her as a bargaining chip to get him to give up the names of the people he's been working for."

Charlotte saw red. "You mean to tell me that a woman's life and reputation are being put on the line just so the FBI can catch some bad guys? That's a load of crap, Martin!"

He lifted his eyes up to hers, and she realized she maybe shouldn't have spoken so strongly to the CEO of the company, but she was mad and wanted him to know it.

"I appreciate your concern for your assistant," he said sternly, "but I need to remind you that you are a market president of Olde Florida Bank, and your loyalties rest with the company."

Charlotte was embarrassed, and the deep blush on her face showed it. Martin had always been good to her, and he wasn't the person she wanted to fight with. It was Special Agent Nicholas Greyson, the son of a bitch, whom she wanted to crucify, but right now the bank had to come first.

After she apologized for her outburst, she and Martin spent the next half an hour working over their speech to her banking team, and by the time everyone started trickling in, they knew just what they needed to say. Talking with her team and encouraging them to stay positive and united with clients and each other was the hardest thing professionally she'd ever had to do, and when it was over, she was exhausted.

At nine o'clock she turned on the TV in the break room and watched the press conference from Tampa with the regional FBI director and of course Nick. His normally clean-shaven face sported a five o'clock shadow, and the chocolate-brown hair that he kept meticulously combed was sticking up on top. To be honest he looked miserable, and that was the only bright spot in Charlotte's day. As far as she was concerned, he had railroaded her friend and lied to her over and over again, and she wanted him to hurt as much as she did.

Shortly after the press conference ended, the news media was in the bank's parking lot, hoping for interviews with both clients and staff. Thankfully the bank-protection department from the home office had already arrived and was keeping journalists at bay. By five o'clock Charlotte's bones ached, and she was exhausted. She called her team together for one more pep talk before they headed out for the weekend.

"I can't tell you how incredibly proud of you I am," she told them, doing her best not to lose her composure. "Today has been rough, and it's going to be a while before it gets better. Before you leave here tonight, I need to remind you of a few things. First of all, no talking to the media. If you're approached, you either walk away or answer, 'No comment.' Bank protection is handling all communications, and none of us wants to say or do anything that might cause a problem for the bank. Second, I hope you all will get away this weekend, as best you can, and distance yourselves from gossipers. This is not our story to share with anyone, and we all need to remember that Carol is our friend and our colleague, and until she's proven guilty, she's innocent. Now go home, get some rest, and I'll see you on Monday morning."

By five thirty everyone had left, and Charlotte made her way to her car. A couple of straggling reporters tried to talk with her, but she held her head high and kept her mouth closed. Afraid that they might try to follow her home, she took a long route through lots of different neighborhoods before finally pulling into her driveway. She even took the time to put her car in the garage, determined to stay holed up all weekend.

As soon as she was safely inside her bungalow, the waterworks started again. She continued to cry while she stripped out of her clothes and put on a pair of yoga pants and a sweatshirt. It was ninety degrees outside, but a block of ice had settled around her heart, and she just couldn't get warm. Food sounded awful, so she brewed herself a cup of Gran's favorite chamomile tea and put her hands around the mug, relishing in the warmth.

Calling Becca was the first thing that came to her mind, but Charlotte wasn't ready to share her feelings yet. Becca had sent her a text earlier that read, "Brad called and told me what's going on. J and I are here for you. Call when you're ready to talk." Just two days ago she had told Becca about the wonderful weekend with Nick and how she thought they might have a real shot this time. Now once again, he had stabbed her in the back, and the knife had gone all the way through to her heart.

Pulling one of Gran's homemade quilts over her, Charlotte had just gotten comfortable on the couch when someone knocked on the door. She didn't know if it was a reporter or a nosy neighbor, so she made no attempt to get up, hoping whoever it was would go away. But the knocking continued. It sounded as if someone was pounding a fist on her door. Then she heard a voice that made her blood boil and run cold, all at the same time.

"Charlotte, open the door. I know you're in there," Nick shouted. "We need to talk." Charlotte took a sip of her tea and let the anger she was feeling come to the surface. The pounding continued, and Nick pleaded, "Please open the door." This time she could hear the emotion in his voice. "At least let me explain. I'm not leaving until you do."

Wrapping the quilt around her shoulders, almost like a cloak of protection, she slowly opened the door and looked over the man who had rocked her world in more ways than one. Nick looked as bad as she felt, but she refused to be swayed. There were dark circles under his eyes, and instead of being their normal beautiful blue, his eyes were stormy and dark. His suit was so wrinkled she was sure he had slept in it, and with his shirt open and his tie hanging around his neck, he looked as if he'd been on a two-day drunk. But damn if he still wasn't gorgeous.

"May I come in?" he asked cautiously. "I don't want to do this in front of your neighbors."

"You know, for a man who's done about everything possible to ruin my life, you have a lot of demands," she hissed, but knowing this conversation didn't need any eavesdroppers, she opened the door and let him in. Nick ran his hand over his face, obviously not sure where to begin, so she helped him out. "You're on the clock, Special Agent, so don't waste my time with any more lies," she spat. "Say what you think you need to say, and leave me alone."

Nick let out a groan and tried to reach for her. "Charlotte…"

"This is a no-contact conversation," Charlotte told him angrily, "and your time is running out, so speak now or forever hold your peace." Realizing that she had used a reference from a marriage ceremony, Charlotte let out a snarky laugh, thinking about how there had been a time when she had allowed herself to imagine the two of them getting married someday.

"You have to know I never meant for any of this to hurt you," Nick said. "This was strictly business."

"Strictly business, you say, well, that makes it all okay then," she snarled, dropping the quilt and crossing her arms over her chest. "I guess the FBI has no morals when it comes to ruining the lives of innocent people, even if it means screwing their boss to get closer to them."

Nick growled. "You're twisting my words, Charlotte. The investigation was just business, but it had nothing to do with us—you have to believe that. Once we started talking again and I saw the way things were heading, I asked to be taken off of the case, but the director said no. This is my job, Charlotte. I work for the government; I don't make the decisions."

"That day you first came to the bank and we talked about your dad's shortfall on his loan, that was all part of your ruse, wasn't it? Does your conscience even bother you a little bit that you dragged your family into your web of lies? Or was that just business too?"

"They knew what was going on," Nick said quietly. "It was the only way for things to work."

"But evidently, I was just collateral damage, because not once did you say anything to me. And just so we're clear, it's *my* job that you fucked over, the one thing in my life I've ever done well. And now you've taken that away from me too, just like you took the last two weeks of my childhood." Charlotte knew she was pushing the envelope with that last comment, but her anger and hurt had festered for twelve years, and she couldn't keep the volcano from erupting. She could see the hurt in his eyes. They had gone from stormy to almost black, but she was not at all prepared for what he said next.

"I love you, Charlotte. I've never stopped loving you, and if you will let me explain everything from the beginning, I know that you will understand."

You could have heard a pin drop the room was so quiet. Charlotte fought for the words to say back. How long she had wanted to hear him say that he loved her, but she couldn't believe him; she wouldn't. "Those are just words, Nick, just empty words. Let me tell you what love looks like to me, because I had it once, but like all my bad mistakes, I let it get away. I had a man, one who was beautiful inside and out, successful, and caring, and I gave him all those *firsts* you wanted so badly. He wanted to take me to New York, even marry me, but I couldn't, because deep inside I was hoping that by some miracle we'd find each other someday. The funny thing is I didn't even know it, but Ryan figured it out, and it broke his heart." Charlotte had never intended to tell Nick about Ryan, but she was angry, and she wanted him to feel the hurt that she was feeling. "And now it's time for you to go."

The look on Nick's face was one of pure devastation, but Charlotte wasn't about to back down. She walked to the door and opened it, letting him know she was serious.

"Don't run away from us again, Lottie," Nick pleaded.

Charlotte threw the final blow then. "There is no us, Nick. I don't think there ever was. Just a girl looking for a fairytale and a guy looking to get in her pants."

Nick shook his head and moved toward the door. He held on to the frame for a moment before turning back for one more look at her, and then he walked out.

All the rage and all the hurt she had felt all day were gone, and in their place was an emptiness like she had never experienced. Tomorrow she would focus on Carol and how to get her out of this horrible situation, but tonight there was only one thing that would soothe the pain. Deciding that walking home might be safer than driving in her current mood, she headed out the back door, her thoughts on Two Scoops and a triple-rich salted caramel malt.

Chapter 69

Now

The malt lay heavy in Charlotte's stomach as she tried to sleep. As good as it tasted going down, she now remembered why she didn't indulge in rich treats anymore. Or maybe part of the ache in her stomach was traveling down from her heart, because the ache there was like nothing she had ever felt.

Sometime after two she fell asleep. Her dreams were anything but sweet, and she woke up covered in sweat, her head pounding in rhythm with her heart. Knowing more sleep was not in the forecast, she threw her legs over the side of the bed and looked at the full moon shining in her bedroom window. Just twenty-four hours ago her life had been turned upside down, but she knew now wasn't the time to wallow in her own misery but to find a way to help Carol. After three mugs of the strongest coffee pods she could find, she was ready for a shower and some research.

The RICO Act, designed to combat organized crime, had been passed in 1970 and allowed for extended criminal penalties for people found guilty. Charlotte knew there was no way Carol was involved in any type of racketeering activity, so what had she done to be included in a federal investigation? Charlotte had never felt comfortable with Carol's brother, Tony, but he was Carol's only family, so Charlotte had tolerated him. She knew he was the catalyst behind the charges against Carol.

After hours on the Internet Charlotte had a plan of action, but she couldn't put it in place until Sunday evening. The arrest of Tony and Carol Neel, as well as the information about where they lived and worked, was all over the web, so as much as Charlotte didn't want to, she needed to talk with her mom. By late that afternoon she had called her mom and Becca, the first call strictly about the arrest and the other a mixture of both professional and personal pain. She'd also received an e-mail from Ryan letting her know he was there if she needed a friend, but that only broke her heart more.

Sunday dragged by. After another night with little sleep she had gotten up early and thrown herself into cleaning mode. Now her little cottage was sparkling, and she was ready to put her free-Carol plan into play. Grabbing a new bottle of chilled Beach House white, she picked up her cell and made the call that she hoped—no, she knew—would start the ball rolling.

"Well, Charlotte Luce," came the voice on the other end, "I thought you were going to delete me from your contacts."

Charlotte groaned. "I guess I deserve that, Peter," she replied cautiously, "but I need legal help, and you're the best lawyer I know."

Peter's demeanor changed immediately. "Are you in trouble?" he asked with sincerity. "I read about your assistant being arrested, but your name wasn't mentioned."

"I'm fine, Peter," she said, "but Carol needs better representation than she'll get from a pro bono attorney, which is why I'm calling you."

"I'm a corporate attorney, Charlotte; you know that. I haven't been a part of a criminal defense since law school. And even if I could help Carol, the firm wouldn't allow me to do it without compensation, and from what I've read, I'm afraid it's going to end up being pretty costly."

Charlotte sighed. "I know you aren't the right lawyer for the case, Peter, but you have to know someone who is. Please, you're the only person I trust to help me. And don't worry about the cost; I'll cover whatever it is." She could almost hear the thoughts going through his mind, so she added, "And yes, Peter, I played right into Nick Greyson's hands, but that's behind me. Getting Carol out of this mess is my focus. I'll beg you if that's what it will take."

Charlotte was thankful that Peter didn't comment on her admission about Nick. "I have a couple of people in mind," he told her, "and I'll give them a call first thing in the morning, but, Charlotte, how do you think the bank will react to you paying for Carol's defense?"

"Honestly, I don't know," she said, "but I can't just sit back and let her be blamed for something I know she wasn't a part of. The bank will either have to support me or fire me; it's their choice."

"I'll let you know when I have some information, but I really want you to think about this, Charlotte. I know Carol was your assistant, but how much do you know about her and her life? I'd hate to see you lose everything you've worked so hard for only to find out that she's guilty."

"Carol isn't just my assistant; she's my friend," Charlotte protested. "And she's not guilty. There's no doubt in my mind about that. But thank you, Peter, for caring and for helping me. I know I don't deserve it."

Charlotte hung up the call and scrolled through her e-mails and texts, curious to see if there were any messages from Nick. Of course Martin had e-mailed her several times, and both the *Tampa Bay Times* and the *Anna Maria Islander* had e-mailed asking for an interview, but there was nothing from Nick. Evidently he had taken her at her word when they talked on Friday night. So why didn't she feel relieved instead of so miserable?

Chapter 70

Now

Monday was a disaster at work, the only saving grace being that Pam returned from her vacation. Clients were calling and coming in with questions all morning long, and by noon Charlotte was ready to explode. Most people were just curious and looking for a juicy story, but others were concerned about their accounts and the soundness of Olde Florida Bank. Not wanting to leave her team alone to deal with the onslaught, Charlotte sat at Carol's empty desk, ready to field anything that came her way.

The normally pleasant voice that she used when talking with customers was about gone when the phone rang yet again shortly after two o'clock. "Thank you for calling Olde Florida Bank," she answered. "This is Charlotte Luce."

"Charlotte," said a confused Peter, "are you manning the phones today?"

Charlotte took a deep breath, not wanting to take out her frustrations on him, and replied, "Just supporting my team, Peter. Please tell me you have good news."

"I think it's good," he told her, "and I hope you will as well. I called my friend Owen Gardner this morning. After reviewing the charges, he's convinced of Carol's innocence, at least in regard to the RICO charges, so he agreed to take her case. The arraignment was scheduled for this morning, but a flu bug shut down the courthouse, so it's been rescheduled. I told him you were good for the retainer, so I hope you haven't changed your mind."

Charlotte smiled for the first time all day. "Thank you so much, Peter. I can't tell you how much this means to me. Just send me the information on Owen and the amount I need to send him, and I'll do a People Pay through online banking right away."

"It was my pleasure, Charlotte, and I look forward to hearing from you again."

Charlotte hung her head. She was so happy to have someone else on Carol's side, but she could hear the *want* in Peter's voice, and the last thing she wanted or needed was to even think about a man. *Shit, shit, shit!*

By Wednesday the gossipmongers had stopped their calls for the most part, and Charlotte was trying to get some real work done. The main office sent her a reserve to fill Carol's position, but she was going to have to start looking for a full-time replacement soon. She was deep in thought when her office phone buzzed and the reserve announced that Mr. Riggs was on the line.

"Martin," Charlotte said, "please tell me you're not calling with bad news. I'm not sure I can take any more right now."

Martin Riggs was a very caring man, but he was also very professional and a good CEO for Olde Florida. He had been Charlotte's champion, but he didn't seem too pleased with her right now. "I received a call from the deputy director of the Tampa office of the FBI today, Charlotte. He seems to think that you've hired an attorney to represent Carol Neel and that you're footing the bill. Please tell me that he's wrong."

"I wish that I could, Martin, but everything he told you is true. I won't let Carol go to prison because of her slimy brother or the unethical agent who's railroading her." Charlotte knew she was treading on thin ice, but she had told Peter the truth: the bank could support her or fire her.

"I'm disappointed to hear that, Charlotte. I was hoping I had made the bank's position clear when I was there last Friday." He waited for

207

her to respond, but Charlotte stayed quiet. He added, "The director mentioned too that you have a personal relationship with the investigating and arresting agent, the one you're accusing of being unethical."

This time Charlotte had to speak up. "We grew up together, right here on the island. It had been twelve years since we'd last seen each other until he came into the bank a few weeks ago. Maybe unethical is a little too strong, but I'm definitely disappointed in his moral character."

Martin thought about her answers and then responded. "I have no choice but to report this to the ethics committee," he explained. "I'm sure you'll be hearing from HR within the next week or so."

Charlotte hated that she was letting Martin down, but someone had to be in Carol's corner, and there was no one to step up but her. If Gran hadn't given her the cottage on the beach, along with lots of years of rental income, she might not have had the resources to help, but thankfully Gran had, and Charlotte knew she needed to pay that gift forward.

Chapter 71

Now

Thursday was another hectic day, and Charlotte was about to tear her hair out. The reserve from the main office needed lots of hand-holding, and Charlotte didn't have the time to keep showing her what needed done and also stay on top of her own work. To make matters worse, one of her long-term tellers had an offage in her cash drawer, and it was large enough that every strap of money in the vault had to be opened and counted by two people. It was a lengthy and tedious process, but the offage was found, which definitely lightened the mood in the already somber banking center.

By the time Charlotte got home from work, it was almost seven thirty, and she was dead on her feet. She never minded working long hours, but twelve hours trying to keep spirits high when her own were sinking, plus worrying about what she would hear from the bank's ethics committee, had worn her down. Not even bothering with dinner, she undressed and climbed into bed, hoping a good night's sleep would give her some clarity.

On Friday morning, as she put on her jeans and her blue Olde Florida Bank shirt, Charlotte had a plan to make things better. She stopped at the bakery on her way to work and bought two maple-pecan coffee cakes for her team as well as a fruit tray from Publix, and she got in early enough to make sure there was plenty of coffee for everyone. These people were more than employees to her, and she was going to make sure they all knew it. She had learned a long time ago that it wasn't just men whose hearts were swayed by food.

At lunchtime she bought subs, chips, and drinks, and for the first time in a week people started to loosen up and get back to normal, at least as normal as they could be under the circumstances. At two o'clock, after the last lunch hour was over, Charlotte sat down at her desk and took a deep breath. She needed to go out on client calls, but the strain of the last week had taken all her energy, and she just couldn't deal with schmoozing yet. A knock on her office door brought her focus back, and Charlotte looked up to see Dan standing in the doorway. "May I come in?" he asked.

"Of course, Dan," she answered. "You know my door is always open for you. What's up?"

"I know this past week has been really rough on you, Charlotte, but I just wanted to thank you for caring so much about your staff. You're a great boss, but you're more than that to us, and I just wanted to tell you how much we all appreciate you."

Charlotte smiled, one of the first real smiles she'd had in over a week, and tried to keep the tears at bay. "All of you are what's kept me going, Dan. You're more than just my staff; you're my family. This whole situation would be unbearable without your support, and your kind words will help me get through, no matter what the future brings."

The conversation with Dan was enough to get her through the rest of the day, but with the weekend looming ahead, Charlotte thought once more about Carol, and it made her blue again. After work she would call Peter and see if he had any new information about Carol's case.

Once she was home and had changed into shorts and a tank top, Charlotte poured herself a big glass of wine and punched in the numbers to Peter's cell. As soon as he answered, she had regrets about calling him, but what choice did she have?

"Hello, Charlotte," he answered. "I was just thinking about you and hoping you'd call this weekend."

Shit, shit, shit, she thought. *I need Peter on my side, but how do I do that without making him think this is anything more than me needing information about Carol?*

"Well, actually I was hoping you might have some news about Carol and what Owen's been able to do. I really need to get his contact information from you, and then I won't have to involve you in this mess," she said, hoping he understood. But no, not Peter!

"I'm happy to be involved," he said. "Why don't we meet for a drink, and I'll tell you everything that I know."

"Um, not tonight, Peter," she hedged. "I'm already in for the evening, and I've had a glass of wine, but thanks for the offer. Do you have Owen's information handy?"

"Maybe another time," he said stiffly. "I'll give Owen your number and have him call you when he has something to share. Good night, Charlotte."

Perfect! Just perfect! She had hurt Peter again when all she wanted to do was help Carol. Just another example of how bad at relationships she was.

The rest of the weekend was long, with only a call from Becca to help Charlotte's downward-spiraling mood. She thought a visit with Mrs. Danvers might help her spirits, but Mrs. D's daughter, Roma, was there, so Charlotte made a quick exit. *Pop would know just what to do,* she thought, and then the realization that she was losing Pop again hit her hard.

"Maybe it was just business, Nick," she said to herself, "but how could you do this to your family?" She genuinely loved Pop, and she knew he loved her, but she would never ask him to choose between her and Nick. That was the whole reason she had stayed away for the past twelve years, and now, when her relationship with Pop had begun again, Nick had ripped it out from under them.

Chapter 72

Now

Waiting to hear from the ethics committee was agonizing, and with every passing hour Charlotte felt a little more and more uncertain. She finally called her mom to let her know what was going on, and surprisingly, her mom was very supportive. "No news is good news, Lottie," her mom told her. "The bank knows what an asset they have in you, and they'll make the right decision."

Charlotte was doing her best to hold on to what her mom had said, but after a week with no word, the discomfort she was feeling kept getting stronger. Realizing she needed to make a game plan, just in case, she made a list of her assets and of what she might do if she lost her job. The first thing she wrote down was a long-overdue visit to her mom.

On Friday afternoon, at about two o'clock, Becca's brother Brad showed up at Charlotte's office looking like death warmed over. He knocked on the door and, without waiting for her to invite him in, sat down in one of the leather chairs across from her desk. The last time a man she knew had looked so terrible, her world had fallen apart, so she knew this wasn't a courtesy visit.

"Brad," she said as she got up and closed her door, "I guess I don't need to ask why you're here or what this is about."

Brad hung his head and looked up at her. "I want you to know that I hate this, and I don't agree with it at all, but the decision has been made that the bank can't afford to retain you, given your admitted financing of Carol Neel's defense, as well as your personal relationship with Special Agent Nicholas Greyson. I'm really sorry, Charlotte."

Even though she had tried to prepare herself for this outcome, it felt like a punch to her gut when the words were finally spoken. She looked at Becca's brother, and her heart went out to him. Brad had done so much for her, and she believed him when he said he didn't agree with the decision, and making things harder for him wasn't in her nature. "It's okay, Brad," she said with a wary smile. "Martin gave me warning as to where my loyalties needed to lie, but to be honest, I never felt I was being disloyal to Olde Florida, just being a friend to Carol. What happens now?"

"Officially we're saying that we have amicably agreed for you to leave the employment of the bank. You'll be given eight weeks' severance pay, as well as pay for the six vacation weeks you have available. You will need to clear out your office and turn in your keys and codes to me today."

Charlotte felt as if she were in a bad dream and kept waiting to wake up. In her mind she said, *Congratulations, Nick, you really fucked me over this time*, but to Brad she said, "That's very generous, Brad, but not necessary. If the bank feels this strongly about terminating me, they certainly shouldn't be trying to hide anything or compensating me in any way. Just fire me and get it over with."

Brad shook his head and leaned toward her desk. "I already feel like shit about this, Charlotte. Please don't make it any harder. Martin Riggs himself put this package together for you, and trust me—he isn't any happier with the committee's decision than I am. But we have shareholders to answer to, and their feeling is that what you're doing is risking our reputation, and we can't afford any more bad publicity over this."

The realization this was really happening hit her, and Charlotte felt sick. Yes, she had said the bank could support her or fire her, but she'd never really thought they would fire her. It wasn't Brad's fault or even

Martin's. She had made the commitment to help Carol, and she was going to see it through.

"I understand, Brad," she finally said, "and I do appreciate everything you and Martin have done for me. I especially appreciate the opportunity you gave me six years ago, and I'm truly sorry I let you down."

"Oh, Charlotte, you haven't let me down. I'm proud of the job you've done here, and I can't tell you how much I respect what you're doing for Carol. Sometimes life just sucks, and this is one of those moments."

Brad stayed around while she packed up the few personal items she had in her office. Then he took her keys and passcodes and gave her a hug. "That hug was for my sister's best friend," he told her, trying to smile, "and not an employee of Olde Florida Bank. And speaking of my sister, she's going to have my ass for this, you know."

"Let me talk with Becca first, okay? I promise that she'll understand and not hold you responsible."

While the lobby was busy, and every staff member was with a customer, Charlotte slipped out the door. At five o'clock Brad was going to tell her team that she and the bank were parting company for personal reasons. She had no doubts that they would figure out the truth, but that was on the bank, not her.

Chapter 73

Now

By the time she got home, Charlotte was a wreck. More than anything she wanted to grab a bottle of wine and climb into bed, but she was determined not to let another setback in her life turn her into a wino. Instead, she changed into comfy clothes and picked up the phone to call Becca. After she poured her heart out to her friend and made sure Becca understood the situation was not Brad's fault, she choked down a container of yogurt and had a heart-to-heart with her gran.

"At least this time I didn't run away," she said as she rubbed her locket. "You always told me to do the right thing, Gran, and I honestly believe that's what I'm doing with Carol. I sure hope you understand."

After a night of restless sleep, Charlotte got up around six on Saturday morning. She knew she should go for a run, but the first thing on her agenda was talking with Owen Gardner and seeing what needed done to get Carol out of jail. Since Peter had been less than helpful in getting her Owen's contact information, she decided to do some Internet research. *I should have just done this in the first place,* she chided herself when the information appeared without much effort.

She knew the law office would be closed since it was Saturday but decided to go ahead and leave a message, just in case voice mails were checked over the weekend. Instead, she was pleasantly surprised when Owen himself answered the phone. "This is Charlotte Luce, Owen," she said. "I'm sorry to bother you on a Saturday morning, but I'm really anxious to hear what's going on with Carol Neel's case. Do you have any updates for me?"

"No need to apologize, Charlotte. I'm an early bird myself, and I'm actually here today working on Carol's case. Now that the judge is well, the court will work on rescheduling her arraignment. I feel confident she'll be released, and I'm hoping to get the charges dropped as well. Her brother is adamant that the only part Carol played in this mess was opening the account he used for his illegal operations. She admits to not following the Enhanced-Due-Diligence procedures and trusting the information her brother gave her, but that's not a criminal offense unless she was involved in the money-laundering scheme, and Tony swears she wasn't."

Charlotte breathed a sigh of relief. "I can't tell you how good that is to hear," she told him. "Carol loves her brother, but I couldn't believe she would do anything illegal for him. The EDD procedure is a big thing with the OCC, but we opened accounts for years without needing to do it. With Carol being a seasoned employee, I'm sure she didn't see the harm in opening the account like she did. That was poor judgment on her part, but, as you said, not a criminal offense. So what happens next?"

"E-mail me all your information, and either my assistant or I will get in touch with you after the hearing. I like Carol a lot. She's genuine and very forthcoming, and I intend to help her all that I can. I'm really glad that Peter thought of me when you went to him for help."

"I'm glad too," she said, "and I'll be anxious to hear from you after her arraignment. Thank you, Owen. Thank you so much."

Charlotte was feeling so much better that she decided to make some muffins and try another visit with Mrs. Danvers. She had just gone into the kitchen to make sure she had a box mix when someone knocked on her front door. Afraid as always it might be Nick or a rogue reporter, she peeked out the window first, and there stood Noah.

She opened the door reluctantly and looked at him without saying a word. The look on his face was one of concern and not his usual playboy demeanor, so when he asked to come in, she stepped aside. Anyway, her issues weren't with Noah but his jackass big brother.

"I went to the bank yesterday afternoon, and Dan told me you'd resigned. There's a mistake someplace, right?" he asked her.

Charlotte shook her head. "Let's just say the bank and I decided to part company."

"Are you telling me they fired you, Lottie? Holy shit, please tell me that didn't happen."

"What happened with me is nothing compared to Carol sitting in jail on some trumped-up charge your brother came up with. I don't turn my back on my friends when they need help, even if he doesn't care how he treats his." She looked up at him defiantly, waiting to see if he would defend Nick.

"I know you're angry, Lottie, and I know that you're hurt, so go ahead and say whatever you need to, and I'll listen. But just so we're clear—I won't talk badly about my brother, no matter what." Noah ran his fingers through hair and then added, "Besides, I need to tell you something that will probably make you just as upset with me, so could we sit down for a few minutes?"

Charlotte led him to the couch but stayed quiet, letting him take the lead.

"Do you remember when Carol and I went out earlier this year?" Noah asked. "We had dinner and were on our way back to her place when she realized she had left the key to her apartment in another purse. She said her brother, Tony, had a spare, so she called him and asked if he would bring it to her. Unfortunately, Tony had been drinking and wasn't in good shape to drive. What else could I do but offer to drive her to his place?"

"Doesn't Tony live out on Longboat Key?" Charlotte asked.

"Yeah, and that's where this clusterfuck started. Tony doesn't just live on Longboat; he lives in one of those gated million-dollar condo communities. I picked Carol up at her apartment, so I knew it was an average apartment in an average neighborhood. Why was Tony living so extravagantly when she lived so modestly? I know that siblings don't have to be equals financially, but from what Carol told me, his livelihood came from doing the books for some local independent businesses, and that didn't jibe with his fancy digs."

Charlotte listened intently and then said, "Tony took care of your dad's books too, didn't he? I remember when his loan payment was late the first time he mentioned checking with Tony."

"Pop was one of them, yes, which is probably why I paid attention in the first place. Anyway, we got the key. By the time we made it back to Anna Maria, it was late, so I took Carol home and left." Noah took ahold of Charlotte's hands and looked her right in the eye. "I'm the one who told Nick I thought there was something off about Tony Neel, Lottie. I called him the next day just to share my observations. He said he couldn't tell me much but asked me to learn more about Tony, so I did. It's me you should be mad at, Lottie, not Nick."

Charlotte could see that he was hurting, so she gave him a kind smile. "You didn't do anything wrong, Noah, and there's a lot more involved in my anger at Nick than his investigation of Tony Neel; you have to know that."

"I do know, but I still feel responsible. I used Carol to get information about her brother, and the FBI used that information in an ongoing investigation on organized crime in the area. I never thought for a minute that what I told Nick would get Carol in trouble, and I would never have been a part of anything I knew would cause you so much pain."

There was so much emotion in his voice that Charlotte couldn't help but put her arms around him. Noah had been another pawn in the FBI's chess game, and she was tired of them yanking around people whom she cared about. "You're a good man, Noah Greyson," she said, giving him a big squeeze. "How can it be that no woman has captured your heart?"

"Who says one hasn't?" he answered quietly.

Charlotte pulled away from their embrace and asked excitedly, "Who is it, Noah? Is it someone I know?" He looked up at her, and when his brown eyes met hers, she had her answer, and her heart ached. "Oh, Noah," she said as she started to cry.

He lifted her chin and smiled down at her. "Don't cry, Shortcake. It's okay, really."

"Does Nick know?" she stammered, almost afraid to hear the answer.

"Sure he does. Why do you think he got so pissed whenever he saw me touching you? You were always Nick's girl, Lottie; I knew there was never a chance for me. But I've got to admit—it was kind of fun torturing him."

Charlotte hung her head, ashamed of how selfishly she'd held on to her hurt, like she was the only person to ever experience it. When Noah left, she was going to call her mom and tell her she was coming for a visit. She was finally ready to leave the past behind and let the Greyson family move forward without her. It might kill her, but it was the right thing to do.

Just then Noah's cell phone rang. He looked down at the caller ID and ignored it. As soon as the ringing stopped, it started again, and this time he answered. "Hey, Pop, what's up?" he said casually into the phone. His back became rigid, and his color changed from summer bronze to ghostly white. "I'll be right there," he said, ending the call.

"What is it, Noah?" Charlotte asked. "What's wrong with Pop?"

He just shook his head, and with tears running down his face he said, "It's Nick, Lottie...

He's been shot."

To be continued in Book Two, *"Call Me Charlotte"*
See the Following Excerpt

Call Me Charlotte

Prologue

I had never felt so much quiet, while being surrounded by so much noise. The sirens were blaring and communications were coming in over the scanner, but squeezed between Noah and Pop, the three of us holding hands, all I could hear were my own thoughts, and they weren't pretty.

"My name is Charlotte Luce and I'm the youngest, and first female market president in the history of Olde Florida Bank. Well I was before they fired me. The bank called it an amicable split, but let's be honest, I was fired. I loved my job with Olde Florida, and I was good at it, but a difference of opinion about my decision to support my assistant after she and her brother were arrested, caused a big stink, so now I'm unemployed.

My gran used to say that things happen for a reason, and I think she was right. There's no way I could be thinking about banking right now because there's a man lying in the hospital, possibly fighting for his life, and there's something he needs to know. I never stopped loving him either."

Scheduled for Release April 2018

About the Author

Dana L. Brown is a long-time banker and graduate of the American Bankers Association School of Bank Marketing and Management, where she earned the distinction of Certified Financial Marketing Professional. She attended Ball State University where she majored in business.

The mother of three daughters, she lives with her husband in Indiana, but loves traveling to the laid-back lifestyles on the beaches of Florida. *Lottie Loser* is her debut novel.

http://www.danalbrownbooks.com/

Facebook: @DanaLBrownAuthor

Twitter: @DanaLBrownBooks